QUEEN OF HEARTS

COLLEEN OAKES

Originally published as *Queen of Hearts:*
Volume One: The Crown in 2014 by Spark Press

This edition published in the USA by HarperCollins Publishers Inc. in 2016
This edition published in Great Britain in 2016 by
HarperCollins Children's Books, a division of
HarperCollins Publishers Ltd,
1 London Bridge Street,
London SE1 9GF

www.harpercollins.co.uk

1

ISBN: 978-0-00-817539-9

Typography by Jenna Stempel

Printed and bound in England by Clays Ltd, St Ives plc

MIX
Paper from
responsible sources
FSC
www.fsc.org
FSC™ C007454

FSC™ is a non-profit international organisation established to promote the
responsible management of the world's forests. Products carrying the FSC
label are independently certified to assure consumers that they come from
forests that are managed to meet the social, economic and ecological needs
of present and future generations, and other controlled sources.

Find out more about HarperCollins and the environment at
www.harpercollins.co.uk/green

"How do you like the Queen?" said the Cat in a low voice.

"Not at all," said Alice: "she's so extremely—" Just then she noticed that the Queen was close behind her, listening: so she went on, "—likely to win, that it's hardly worth while finishing the game."

— Alice's Adventures in Wonderland *by Lewis Carroll*

One

"Oh, my future queen, you're late!" Harris hopped from one foot to the other, his plump face soaked with a cold sweat. He pulled off his thick-rimmed glasses and wiped them on his white checkered ascot. "Dinah! Walk faster, Your Highness! We are late, late, late!" He looked down at his pocket watch with an exaggerated sigh.

Dinah, Princess of Wonderland and future Queen of Hearts, rolled her eyes.

"Harris, I'm walking as swiftly as I can."

"With all due respect, my dear, we have a very important

summons from the King of Hearts. Your father wishes to see you. You know he is not a patient man."

Dinah continued to shuffle down the Hallway of the Golden Birds feeling quite like one of the ridiculous bronze fowl perched on the golden pedestals that surrounded her.

A little bird ran across her path, and Dinah stomped near its feet, sending it shrieking into the air.

"My child!" thundered Harris. "Control your emotions! I beg of you—do not let your father see that behavior or you will be sleeping in the Black Towers."

"I doubt it," snipped Dinah glumly. "I wish that would happen, because then I would get to see inside them."

Harris gave Dinah a disappointed look. "Never wish yourself inside the Black Towers," he said gravely. "You have no idea the evil that lurks there."

Dinah considered slowing her pace just to annoy him but took pity on her guardian and tutor, the man who had raised her from childhood. Harris had once been a dashing Card, or so Dinah had heard, but now he was somewhat walrus-like, a portly man with white hair and a dozen varieties of checkered outfits. Without a doubt, he loved

Dinah deeply—something she lacked in other areas of her life. Dinah raised her voice, its sharp tone bouncing off the ornate halls of Wonderland Palace.

"Why should I have to go to the Great Hall? I never get to say anything, and Father won't even talk to me." *Or look at me*, she thought.

Harris patted her roughly on the head. "You shouldn't say such things about the King of Hearts."

Annoyed, the Princess of Wonderland turned her head as she walked past a bright, open balcony, breathing in the fresh air that filtered in between red panes of glass.

Her black eyes could make out the various landmarks of Wonderland spread out like the threading of a distorted quilt—the horizon that would soon be hers to govern and rule. Dinah allowed herself a deep breath of pleasure as her eyes hungrily ate up everything in sight. To the north stretched endless fields of wildflowers, and eventually, the Ninth Sea, though she had never seen it. Beyond that, she knew from her studies, were the dreaded Caves of Mourning and the Todren, home to mermaids and sea monsters, of children's tales and nightmares. To the east, beyond the plains, she could vaguely make out the topless Yurkei Mountains that lay past the Twisted Wood, where adventurers went to die at the hands of the brutal Yurkei Mountain tribes. To the south lay the Darklands, a place of untold horrors.

Closer to her was Wonderland proper: small towns, roads, windmills, and rivers that sat just beyond the iron palace gates. This was *her* country—the heart of Wonderland, as far as the eye could see. Dinah raised her arms as if to embrace it all.

Harris snapped his watch open. "Stop dillydallying, child! You do not want the king to be even angrier than he already is."

Dinah gave her body a final shake in the sun and sullenly sped her pace, her feet tripping on the hem of the ornate and ridiculous dress she had been forced to wear. The high, stiff collar of the dress was lined with hard gemstones that bled down her chest in a wild pattern that made her neck itch.

Dinah hated this dress. Dinah hated *all* dresses.

Her ebony hair was twisted up in an insufferably tight bun, one that exaggerated Dinah's already-large black eyes.

Upon her head sat the princess crown—a thin string of red ruby hearts outlined in gold spikes. Even though it was thin, it was still heavy. It glittered in the sunlight, and it was the only thing Dinah was wearing today that she liked. On her feet twinkled a pair of molded white slippers, inlaid with tiny white diamonds. Before her mother, Queen Davianna, died, she had taken up the lady's hobby of slipper making. Dinah hated the way the petite stones cut into her toes and heels.

Dinah and Harris approached the Great Hall. Two vast ivory doors loomed terrifyingly before her, elaborately carved with the history of Wonderland. Wicked trees, dead Yurkei warriors, and the four symbols of the Cards danced on the wood. She stopped walking and closed her eyes.

Perhaps, she thought, *perhaps if I wish really hard, I could be anywhere but here.*

Two Heart Cards, both handsome men, sharp and crisp in their red-and-white uniforms, opened the doors for them as they approached.

Dinah felt her knees begin to shake and she froze. *Not now, oh gods, not now.*

She felt Harris's hand on her shoulder, and she was

grateful for the calming effect it bestowed. He bent down and looked the princess directly in the face. "Dinah, my child, the king has called you here for a very special reason. He is your father, and he rules over this kingdom. Try to remember that. Everything the king does is for Wonderland."

Dinah's heart was hammering wildly in her chest. Something was wrong, she could sense it.

Harris licked his wrinkled finger and wiped something from her face. "Dinah, look at me. Everything will be fine. I'll be waiting for you out here."

Dinah was seized by a sudden panic. She grabbed his hand and squeezed. "No. I want you to come in with me."

"I am not allowed in the Great Hall for this . . . just for today. The king desires your full attention."

Harris had never been excluded from an event in the Great Hall. As her guardian, he was welcome even to observe the King's Council. But not today.

"*No!*" Dinah flung her arms around Harris. "Please come. I don't know what's going on, please, just come with me."

Harris detached Dinah from his thick waist. "Dinah! Do not forget who you are. You are the Princess of Wonderland. Would you like to embarrass the king?"

Dinah shook her head. "No."

"Then go in there and greet him in the respectful way." He gave her a generous smile. "It will be all right, child. Trust me. Now put on your brave face. Let me see it."

Dinah scowled.

"No, that's not it. Show me *brave* Dinah. Dinah the fearless, the future Queen of Wonderland, the future Queen of Hearts."

Dinah took a deep breath and steeled her black eyes. She stood up taller and sucked in her belly.

"There, that looks a little bit better." Harris patted her head happily, but Dinah was sure that she spotted tears in his weathered eyes. "It's time. We are very late, my dear. I'll be out here."

With that, he pushed her gently into the hall. The ivory doors slammed shut behind her, the sound bouncing around the vast room. Voluminous red banners billowed from floor to ceiling, a black heart stitched across each center: the blazon of the king. Dinah's white slippers echoed loudly against the marble floors, and she felt thousands of eyes watching her, judging her. She held her crowned head as highly and regally as she could. The entire court watched her walk up the aisle, lords and ladies of noble birth, their bright fashion a blot of color on the otherwise black-and-white marble room. Dinah walked swiftly toward the thrones, but the front of the Great Hall still seemed to be miles away.

The different factions of Cards all nodded their heads as Dinah passed, some saying "Princess" under their breath. She heard a faint snicker and an insulting whisper from a Diamond Card. "Discard."

She held her head high and straight, as Harris had told her to do. *Someday this will be my Great Hall*, she told herself. *All these Cards will bow before me when I rule beside my father.*

All the Cards were in attendance today, a rare sight. There were four divisions of the men called Cards, each serving their purpose to the kingdom. Heart Cards, handsome and skilled men uniformed in red and white, protected the royal family and the palace. Club Cards, dressed in gray, were in charge of administering justice: they punished criminals and murderers and organized Execution Day. Their most important function was running the Black Towers. Diamond Cards, clad in vibrant purple cloaks, protected and managed the treasury and sought to increase the king's resources. And then there were the Spades. Spades were the warriors, those in charge of fighting and pillaging. The Spades scared Dinah; cloaked in black, they were hard, grizzled men with dangerous pasts. They were viewed as untrustworthy, brutal, and bloodthirsty. If criminals were reformed and pledged their fealty, they were allowed to join the Spades; that is, if they didn't die in the Black Towers first.

The Spades were universally loathed and feared across Wonderland. Her father held a firm hand over them, but he was the first king to overpower them with his iron fist. He had executed their strongest leaders and subdued their wildness. The Spades simmered quietly, like a burning ember that could ignite and spread over the entire city. All the Cards, though, no matter how frightening, were the source of much lore and many legends. When Dinah was a child, she loved to lie in her raised bed at night and list the Cards in her favorite order: Hearts first, since they protected her, then the Diamonds, then the Clubs, and finally the Spades.

"DINAH!" A loud voice bellowed from the king's throne, and Dinah felt a tiny trickle of sweat roll down the side of her forehead. She had been lost in thought, standing midaisle. Dinah bowed her head. "Get up here. Now."

She walked quickly to the platform, up a set of wide stone steps. Atop the platform sat two massive chairs. They were carved from gold, each in the shape of a large heart. From the top of the thrones, tiny hearts rose upward, growing smaller and sharper the higher they reached. The tops ballooned out and opened into a flurry of sculpted hearts, as if they were taking flight. They reminded Dinah of birds. The pair of heart thrones was a part of Wonderland history: for it was said that once you sat in the king's throne, magic funneled down through the open hearts and made you wise.

Looking at her father, she knew that wasn't true.

One of the thrones sat empty, a lone red rose always upon it. Davianna, her mother, had died when Dinah was a small girl. The second throne was commandeered by her father. The King of Hearts stood before her now, a giant man full of fury and righteousness and an insatiable lust for food and women. As his blue eyes lingered angrily on Dinah's face, she saw him the same way his people did: he was the kind of king who would sooner ride into battle on his Hornhoov than rule from behind the council table. He was a man of action, a brutal and brave man whose rage was legendary. The people of Wonderland respected the king, but only because he represented a force to be reckoned with . . . and feared. What mattered to the townspeople was that he kept them safe from the Yurkei, and that was worth everything. Dinah didn't believe he was a great king, but even she knew better than to ever speak those words. As she looked upon the king's hard face, she remembered the time she had mentioned this to Harris, who had given her a hard shake.

"Don't ever say that about the King of Hearts!" he had cried. "Do you wish to be beheaded?"

"No," she cried hysterically, "I only want him to notice me!"

Harris had held her close that day, stroking her hair. "He will never be the father you deserve," he whispered. He brought Dinah her favorite tart and then they watched the sunset from the croquet green, a rare treat.

"If he wasn't king," Dinah sniffled, "maybe he would love me."

"Oh, child," replied Harris, "that is not to be. Your father is a brutish man and unsure of his place in his child's life, even when your mother was still alive. Queen Davianna was all he had, the only thing he ever desired more than the rush of battle and the smell of fresh blood on his Heartsword. Their relationship had a terrible end, and I fear somehow he blames you."

Dinah thought of this now in the Great Hall as she knelt awkwardly before the thrones. The king's adviser and head of the council, a Diamond Card named Cheshire, bent and whispered soft words in his ear. Dinah's stomach gave a lurch at the sight of him. She did not trust Cheshire. The king growled back at him and then gave a sigh and rose to greet her.

"Dinah, my daughter, my eldest child. I see you are wearing your mother's shoes." Dinah felt a flush rise in her cheeks. *He noticed!* she thought. The king cleared his throat. "Look up at me."

She yanked her head up too quickly, and the crown slipped sideways off her head and landed with a clang on the marble. She saw a frown cross his face.

"Don't be so eager," he hissed quietly. "You look ridiculous with that wanting face."

Dinah felt her lower lip quiver. She clamped her teeth down on it, drawing sweet red blood that she sucked into her mouth. He knelt and picked up the crown, such a diminutive thing in his large hand. He placed it back on her head with a strained smile. The crowd gave a courteous laugh, unaware of his seething anger. The king stood, his long red cloak framing his massive, bull-like figure.

"My daughter, councillors, lords and ladies of the court, Cards, and citizens, it is time for your king to tell you a great truth." He looked down at Dinah. "Sit," he said to her and her alone.

Dinah tried to kneel like a lady should, but she ended up plopping on the floor with a hard breath. She stared up at him, intimidated by his powerful tone. She looked around. There was not a face in the room that was not held in rapt attention by his booming voice.

"Fourteen years ago, we were embroiled in a devastating war with the Yurkei tribe. Mundoo and his warriors were raiding the outer villages of Wonderland, killing and murdering innocent citizens. As the king, I could not let that evil abide. As you might remember, I took my best Hearts and Spades through the Twisted Wood and up to the hills, where we smashed the barbaric tribe and sent Mundoo screaming back into his mountains. It was a great day for Wonderland, a great day for the safety of my people."

The crowd clapped and cheered until the king looked down solemnly, and then they grew suddenly silent. He was able to command a room by his moods alone, Dinah noted—something to remember when she was queen one day.

"We lost many brave Cards that day. I hope that what I confess today will bring them some sort of honor."

An uncomfortable feeling was churning its way through Dinah's stomach as she sat at the base of the thrones. Her heart was clutching itself, giving singular, hard thumps that made loud noises when they met her chest. The king continued on.

"War is bloody and brutal, a thing that can rip through

the very heart of men. War can make a man question everything he believes in, every truth that he holds dear. Wonderland has never seen war, so allow me to confess that war can make a man . . . lonely."

The crowd nodded along sympathetically, and in the corner a woman burst into tears. Dinah imagined shaking her until she was quiet. The king had them in his grasp. His dark blue eyes, deep like the sea, blazed with pride.

"As our laws dictate, one might ask for forgiveness for a mistake made during a time of war. I had been away from my dear wife, Davianna, for too long. Gods rest her heart."

The entire crowd, including Dinah, made the sign of a heart over its chest.

"She was the love of my life, and when I left for war, I never imagined it would take so long to return to her. And to my eternal shame . . ." The crowd waited with bated breath as those in the Great Hall stood still. "Gods forgive me, I strayed outside of my marriage vows."

There was a sharp intake of breath from the room; Dinah gasped as well.

"It was a late night, after the battle, and I had drunk a

large bottle of tart wine. Outside my tent, I met a woman from a local village at the base of the mountains. She was kind and generous, and she reminded me so much of my Davianna. My judgment was impaired, and I was grief-stricken for my lost men. We shared that night together, and in the morning I awoke to instant, blinding regret. How could I have betrayed my beloved Davianna? What kind of king was I?" There was a pause.

"That night I found a nearby cliff and prepared to throw myself over."

There was another sharp gasp, and murmurs erupted in the Great Hall. Two women fainted and had to be carried out by Heart Cards. The king gave a sly smile toward his adviser Cheshire, whose rich purple cloak draped over his thin shoulders. Cheshire gave him a quick wink. Only Dinah was close enough to see the exchange.

"As I stood on the edge of the precipice, looking at the changing stars one last time, I swore that I heard a woman singing over the breeze. Something sang me into a deep and dreamless sleep. The next morning, when I rolled over, I was a different man. My will to live had returned. I couldn't shake the feeling that I had met this common and low-born woman for a purpose. I immediately returned to the village to find her, but she had disappeared. I looked everywhere, and I would have kept looking if Mundoo and a small army of his riders hadn't raided our camp that very afternoon. It was chaos. Arrows were flying everywhere, but the maiden was nowhere to be seen. We fought and won, though so many more Cards were lost. Fourteen long years have passed, and there hasn't been a single day when I haven't thought about that woman and wondered what became of her."

The king stomped down the steps, passing Dinah without a single glance. "My loyal subjects, I tell you the truth: a fortnight ago, a mad, raving beggar came to the palace. He had come to sell something priceless and refused to leave until I spoke with him. It was late, and I was furious at being woken. I met him in this very hall, though it was empty and silent as a tomb. Imagine if you will, a king in his royal pajamas meeting a beggar carrying a very large sack. I commanded him to open the sack immediately or a Heart Card would be glad to take his head. Truly terrified, he unrolled the sack . . . and out came a tiny girl."

The crowd sat forward, titillated, including Dinah. Her heart felt like it would explode in her chest.

"She was starving, a pitifully lovely creature, but when she stood and faced me, I saw greatness. I saw—" He paused again for dramatic effect.

"My lost daughter, Vittiore."

Two

The Great Hall erupted in a cacophony of sounds, though Dinah sat stunned and speechless. The king's subjects were screaming and shouting, their tears and applause all dissolving into a wave of happy noise. The king stood still as the crowd rocked and swayed before him. After a few moments, he cleared his throat.

"There could be no mistake that this girl was mine. She had my golden hair, my blue eyes, and the gentle demeanor of her mother, who sadly met her untimely death at the hands of the Yurkei tribes. Since Vittiore has arrived at the palace, I have done nothing but watch and study her, to see if she is truly mine. She has been inspected and interrogated. Though I believed it in my heart, I did not dare to hope it true—until I spoke with her and saw my own reflection in her eyes. Make no mistake: this is my second daughter, who will join her half sister, Princess Dinah, as the Duchess of Wonderland. I will declare it openly, and let no man say otherwise, for he would call the king false and would spend the rest of his life in the Black Towers!"

The King of Hearts let his eyes linger on Dinah, kneeling before him, her body frozen in shock.

"With that, it is my joy and a father's greatest pleasure to introduce to you the Duchess Vittiore."

From behind the king's throne, a small, luminous girl stepped forth. She was young—perhaps fifteen at the most—but already radiant as the sun. Golden curls the color of honey cascaded to her waist, and her bright blue eyes shimmered with happiness and curiosity, her face perfectly unblemished—a picture of innocence. On top of the nest of curls rested a low crown made of sapphire bluebirds, no doubt crafted recently by the palace jewelers. Her long white-and-blue dress brushed the floor, as if she were a maiden on her wedding day.

"Darling," said the king gently. The crowd gasped at her beauty, and one lady-in-waiting fell to her knees with emotion. The king gestured for Vittiore to stand before Dinah. A jealous fury rose in the princess, black and strange. Her hands shook as she gripped the edge of the steps. Her father's booming speech continued.

"Many of you have wondered what you are doing here today. There are no wars to fight, no great matters at hand. It is because I wanted *my* kingdom to know that Wonderland has a *new* duchess, and the joyous ceremonies to celebrate her arrival may begin!"

The hall erupted with a deafening cheer and the ground beneath them gave a shudder with the stomping of feet. The sound rose up like a wave, crashing over Dinah, drowning her. She tried to stand, but her body lurched forward so violently that she slipped down two of the marble stairs, her knees and chest hitting the hard stone with a loud *crack*. Her face flamed red as the entire kingdom watched her—the dark, clumsy princess—who now appeared as a stout donkey next to Vittiore's shining mare. The king gave a chuckle, but there was maliciousness in his eyes as he grasped Dinah roughly by the arm, yanking her to her feet.

"Of course, she will join my two other children, Princess Dinah, my oldest, the future Queen of Hearts, and Charles, her younger brother, the pride of my heart."

Lies, thought Dinah, willing the hot tears flooding her eyes to stay put. *He speaks lies.*

"It is my prayer and my command that this kingdom will embrace my daughter as their new Duchess of Wonderland. If I so much as hear any whispers of the word 'bastard,' those men or women will lose their heads to my Heartsword."

With a labored breath, Dinah twisted her arm out of her father's grasp. She could feel the attention of the crowd focus on her, thousands of mouths hungry for gossip watching her every move. Her black eyes shining like simmering coals, she stared down at Vittiore. The waif with the blond hair took a timid step toward Dinah. Dinah watched her warily, unsure what to do. She felt like screaming and hurling something at her, but she didn't dare. The girl reached out her petite hand.

"My sister," she whispered with a hint of pleading. The crowd inhaled. Dinah met the girl's blue eyes with a furious scowl, and raised her head to the King of Hearts.

"Thank you, Father. I shall welcome her gladly into our . . . family." She choked on her last word. She grabbed the girl's warm hand in her cold one and gave a hard squeeze. The hall erupted in music and cheers as everyone bowed before the two girls and their father. The king saw that the moment he had been waiting for had arrived.

"I invite you all to join us for a celebratory dinner feast in the Dining Hall!" he announced.

The crowd quickly began dispersing, hungry for the piles of tarts and steaming meat that no doubt awaited it. Dinah took a step backward toward the stairs, happy to be released, fearful that her father would see her cry.

"Not you," growled the king, pulling her back, his hand clasped tightly around her arm. Dinah let out a whimper.

"What was that?" he hissed. "Why aren't you happy to meet your new sister?"

Dinah spun around to face him. The tears that she had been holding spilled out over her nose and chin. "What about my mother? I thought . . . I thought . . . ," she whispered.

The king's face lit up with fury and, muttering angrily, he dragged her away from the eyes of the crowd, back behind the thrones, so large they concealed both of them. He grabbed her chin in his hands and held it close, the scent of wine washing over her face from his hot breath. "I never want you to mention your mother again, not in front of Vittiore. Davianna's name will not be spoken in these halls."

Dinah gave a sharp cry. The king's face was growing red.

"STOP IT! STOP CRYING! You need to be glad today, you ungrateful wretch! You have a sister. Be happy."

He was shaking her violently now, and she felt her knees begin to buckle. Suddenly, a long, thin hand curled over the king's shoulder.

"Your Majesty, allow me to deal with her. Princess Dinah has no doubt had an emotional day. I'm sure this is quite a shock for her."

Cheshire, the king's adviser, slithered into view. His face was long and flexible, as if he had no underlying bone structure. He had thick black hair and black eyes. His pale lips were almost the same shade as his skin; but you never saw them, for they were always curled back in a smile, baring his enormous white teeth. Even when Cheshire was smiling and friendly, he looked dangerous. Lean and sinewy, he towered over the king, radiating malice. He was dressed as he always was, in a plum-colored velvet vest and breeches over black boots. A white sash with each Card symbol draped from his left shoulder to the floor, denoting his authority over all the Cards. There was no one above Cheshire but the king. A brilliant purple cloak poured over his hard shoulders.

Dinah stared up at Cheshire with confusion. He was never her ally; rather, he was a man who constantly whispered twisted secrets in her father's ear. The rumors of his extracurricular activities ran rampant in the castle. Some said he spent time in a secret laboratory in the Black Towers, making new species of birds and concocting poisons. Some said he could change forms and wandered the castle all night disguised as a house cat. Dinah had always passed that off as commoner silliness, but now she wasn't so sure. There was a compelling strangeness about him, something that drew her toward his silky promises. Still, she hated him and always had. She blamed him for her father's hatred of her.

Cheshire's voice was gentle as he released the king's fingers from Dinah's shoulders. "I'll take her back to her quarters. Perhaps Princess Dinah isn't feeling up to a feast today."

The king walked away from her without a second glance and curled his arm protectively around Vittiore, who had stood silently through the exchange. She stared back at Dinah with empty eyes.

"Yes, Cheshire. That sounds good. Take her away. Get her out of my sight."

The King of Hearts emerged from behind the thrones and began introducing Vittiore to his many lords and ladies clustered at the base of the stairs. Dinah felt hollowed out, a bowl scraped bare, and so she allowed her father's devious adviser to lead her down a few stairs behind the thrones and out a secret door usually used for the king to take his privy leave. They walked halfway down the stone hallway when Cheshire stopped. Turning toward her with a dangerous smile, he pulled back an elaborate wall tapestry near the privy. Dust showered down on them both, but once it cleared, it revealed a door the same shade as the stone around it. Cheshire held a finger to his lips and with an outstretched hand pushed the door open to reveal a passageway carved into the castle walls.

Dinah was too upset to be impressed, although normally she would have been fascinated. There were many secret ways through Wonderland Palace, and she loved discovering them one at a time. Mostly her days were filled with mind-numbing croquet, etiquette, history, and dancing lessons, but once in a while she was able to slip away from Harris's watchful eye and explore the palace with Wardley.

With a frown, she granted Cheshire a raised whisper as she wiped a stray tear away from her eye. "Where does it go?" asked Dinah.

He was silent.

"Where does it go?" she asked again, annoyed.

He simply nodded his head in the direction of the tunnel. Dinah ducked under the door, her heart hammering equally with dread and curiosity. After a few swift turns down mud-caked stairs, they ended up in a damp stone passage lit by glowing pink lanterns. The twists seemed endless. Cheshire talked quietly as they walked, the high lilt of his voice echoing off the walls.

"I'm sure this was hard for you today, Your Highness. Not only are you getting a younger and much more beautiful sister in your sixteenth year of life, but you heard a clear tale of your father's infidelity to your dear mother, gods rest her heart. An intelligent girl like you can't be surprised. Your father's *desires* for other women are well-known." Cheshire paused, stroking his long chin. "He did not deserve Davianna."

"Don't speak of my mother to me, not now. And she's not my sister," snapped Dinah. "She's a bastard child."

Cheshire's thin fingers wrapped around her elbow, and she found herself yanked backward, face-to-face with him, their noses inches from touching. His lips curled back in anger, revealing his hungry white teeth.

"Listen to me, Dinah," he hissed. "You must *never* let the King of Hearts hear you say that. Things are going to change for you, child, and you had better be made of stronger stuff than the whiny brat you are now. You may be almost of age to be queen, but you are hardly ready."

Dinah twisted her body back from his. "I don't know

what you are talking about," she replied, her voice wavering. "And I don't care. That girl is *not* my sister, and you are not Harris. You know nothing about me. Where is he? Where is Harris?"

"Harris is not here, not that he would be of much use to you outside of tutoring and picking out your gowns in the morning. He does not know about this passage. No one does. Just you and me. There might come a time when it will be of use to you, I am sure. There are many curious things in Wonderland Palace and the Black Towers." He raised an eyebrow at her. "You had best learn everything you do not already know, Princess. Up until now you have been a spoiled girl who spends her days playing in the stables or making doe eyes at Wardley Ghane. Wonderland is a much darker and more twisted place than you imagine."

Something inside Dinah broke. She could take no more of his ridiculous cryptic warnings or his venomous smile. It occurred to her that he was probably here on an errand from the king, to scare her into accepting Vittiore.

"Why are you talking to me?" she snapped. "You don't know anything about me! Leave me be! Please!"

Spinning quickly away from Cheshire, she plunged into the dark tunnel ahead, not looking where she was running, not caring. She was sprinting now, her breathing heavy, her footsteps echoing through the darkness. She turned once and then again, spinning deeper and deeper into the depths of the tunnel, until all she could smell was earth and cold. Cheshire disappeared into the darkness behind her, his calls for her fading quietly into the black. She sprinted beneath the depths of the palace as fast as her jeweled feet could carry her. She turned right, then left, then slipped through a vertical slit in the wall. The dancing pink flames of the lanterns dimmed gradually as the tunnel deepened.

Dinah wasn't thinking—only running, running as fast as she could. She kept seeing her father's proud gaze at Vittiore and the devastated expression on Harris's face as he let her walk into the Great Hall. The tunnel narrowed, and through her tears Dinah could see the stone walls closing in on her. Close to hysterics, Dinah knelt on the cold floor and let the tears wash out, a pouring sob that was deafeningly loud in the tight space. Weeping and pounding on the stone, she let out a loud scream of anger.

How dare he? How dare he be unfaithful to my mother? How dare he bring me in front of the court only to shame me? Why does he hate *me so much?*

In her mind, she saw Vittiore. Vittiore, her new sister, the bastard of her father's loins, the proof that he didn't love her mother as he claimed so publicly. Vittiore, with her long blond hair and cornflower-blue eyes. Dinah raked long furrows into the damp earth. She vowed to herself that she would never befriend Vittiore. She would not speak to her unless forced, and she would not see her perfectly formed face if she could avoid it. It would never be. Speaking to Vittiore would be a betrayal of her mother. *Her mother . . .*

Great heaving sobs escaped her lips, and she was grateful, for once, to have no servants nearby. Here, it was just her and the dirt. She gradually calmed, the darkness like a heavy blanket draped across her wide shoulders. Dinah wiped her eyes and looked around. All was silent. She decided to wander farther. The tunnel grew colder as it went deeper—the air blowing around her had a bitter bite to it. Thick black roots, twisting like snakes, grew overhead. They reminded her of witch's bones, and more than once, she swore she could see them moving and reaching toward her when she looked away. This was a place of dark things.

Dinah stopped a minute to catch her breath. A single lantern lit a passageway in front of her, the flame sputtering in the darkness. She walked through the opening, and in a few steps she came to a round patch of dirt framed by three archways. Each led into a tunnel, and standing in the middle of the circle, Dinah couldn't remember out of which one she had just come. They all looked the same, each lit by a single pink torch. There were symbols etched into the keystone above each opening: a heart, a tree, and one that she didn't recognize—a triangle with a wavy bottom. The sea? She peered at it again. *It must be a mountain*, she thought. The Yurkei Mountains.

Dinah ran her fingers over the symbols. They were thinly raised up from the stone, almost invisible to the naked eye. Her heart pounded in her chest, and the thought of her father discovering her decomposed body when she couldn't find her way back brought Dinah a surprising rush of joy. She furrowed her brow and stared back at the carvings. After a moment, she bent down and peered into the heart tunnel.

Yes—she could see her footprints in the dirt. She let out a sigh of relief. That was the way she had come. It made sense after all; she was the Princess of Hearts. Letting her curiosity lead her, Dinah ventured into the archway that featured the tree symbol. It was even more crooked than the way she had come, and the tunnel kept shrinking until Dinah had to crouch to fit into it, her head brushing the dirty ceiling. It compressed again, and she found herself crawling. The tunnel wound down in a seemingly never-ending curve. White moss began creeping across the walls, and all sounds of palace life ceased overhead. Then, when Dinah felt she couldn't possibly crawl any farther, it opened up into a dusty stone wall, held in place by bolts as thick as her arm. A dead end.

Dinah stood and wrapped her arms around herself, attempting to halt the shivers that shook her shoulders. How long had she been in these tunnels? Time had somehow become irrelevant. Hours? Days? Cold air wafted around her, twisting down from above and shifting the dirt under her feet. She raised her hands above her head and felt fresh air kiss her fingertips. Dinah's eyes followed the bolts upward until they rested on a faintly outlined circle far above her head, its dusty handle barely visible.

A door. Her eyes widened. *These aren't bolts, they're a ladder!* Dinah climbed six bolts before her feet caught on her dress and she tumbled violently to the tunnel floor, scraping her knees and palms.

On her next attempt, she left her dress and shoes behind. Grunting and sweating with the effort and wearing only a slip, Dinah pulled herself to the topmost bolt and pushed against the door. Dust showered her as the door creaked with resistance. Using all her strength, Dinah bent her head and pushed with her shoulders, praying that her feet would not slide from the bolts. Once she did that, the door easily opened, mud and grass raining down on her from above and coating her eyelashes.

With strenuous effort, Dinah heaved herself out through the hole. She sneezed a few times and looked around in fascination as she lay on the ground, feeling her ribs contract. Above her, the Wonderland stars twinkled and, if you watched closely, inched through the sky ever so slightly. Constellations in Wonderland were never constant, and Dinah loved seeing the changing patterns from night to night—circles, spirals, lines, clusters—the stars never formed the same arrangement twice. And here they were, her stars, so bright they lit up all Wonderland. Never had she been so glad to feel the cool breeze on her skin. She only now realized that she had been afraid in the tunnels. Her rage had made her blind. Crisp night air caressed her body. The night breeze dried her tears and cleared her mind.

Once her breathing returned to normal, Dinah stood up and took in her surroundings. She was outside the palace gates, maybe half a mile from the perfect circle of imposing ornamental iron walls that surrounded her home. The infamous iron walls were made of thousands of sharp iron hearts, twisting together in a dance of beauty and defense that warned intruders to stay away. She was facing east now, and if she squinted, she could see the outline of the Twisted Wood, many, many miles away from Wonderland Palace.

She looked down at her toes and wiggled them in the wildflowers blooming around her feet. Somewhere nearby, just inside the gates, the great Julla Tree creaked in the wind, and then a high-pitched wail rippled through the air, alive and intense all at once. It seemed to be laughing at her.

Dinah faced the castle and willed herself not to fear what lay unseen in the open fields behind her. She began walking slowly away from the tunnel.

She had never been beyond the gates of Wonderland Palace, and she gazed upon her palace now, an outsider looking in. It rose out of the fields of red flowers like a beacon of blinding hope. Its golden spires twisted and pierced the sky, the turrets and raised rose gardens adding beauty to its numerous walls, white bridges connecting one tower to the next. Dinah knew that below the turrets, stretching out from the Royal Apartments, was the Croquet Lawn—an endless expanse of green turf, perfect for picnics, croquet, or ostrich riding. Parallel to the Croquet Lawn on the other side of the castle was the Checkered Courtyard. This was where the Spades and Heart Cards lined up for training, and where traitors were executed, their blood spilling across a long, white marble block.

From where she stood, she could barely see anything except the gates and the towering heights of the Royal Apartments. She spied her own bedroom balcony and waved, thinking for a moment that maybe Harris could see her. But he could not. No one knew where she was, and she certainly couldn't tell them about her secret tunnel to the outside. Perhaps, she thought, Cheshire didn't know about the tree tunnel that led to the outside. It was hers alone. There had been no other footprints inside that tunnel, and dust didn't form overnight. There must be another tunnel down there, she thought, one that led to the Royal Apartments. That's where Cheshire had been taking her.

With a smile, Dinah took in the view of the palace one last time. Her castle was a beauty, a fierce and formidable fortress, lovely and dangerous all at once. *One day*, Dinah thought, *this will all be mine*.

I will be the Queen of Wonderland. I will be the queen, and Vittiore will only be the duchess. The thought was enough.

Her knees gave a shake as she stared up at the castle, and Dinah realized that she was exhausted. Her bedchamber seemed very appealing, and the low moan that rose from the Twisted Wood sent shivers down her spine. Dinah took a few steps back to the tunnel entrance, only this time she couldn't find the opening. She knew it had been near some herb plants and a thick, gnarled bush, but it was gone.

Dinah grew more and more aggravated as she paced the area, scuffling dirt and wildflowers aside until she resorted to searching with her fingers through the low grass, illuminated only by the light of the stars. Finally, her fingers found an unnatural groove in the grass and she gave a tug. Nothing happened. Using all the strength left inside her, Dinah heaved. The door didn't move. A trace of fear flashed in Dinah's brain. She pulled again. Her fingernails cracked and broke as the door shuddered and snapped back into place. It wouldn't budge. It was locked. Dinah stared at the door. The wind died down just for a moment, but it was enough. She heard a faint sigh followed by a ragged breath. A torch flared between the door cracks—a tiny sliver of light escaped. Someone was down there. Someone had locked her out. Her breath caught in her lungs. Someone was waiting for her. The Twisted Wood gave another loud moan, the sound carrying for hundreds of miles. Dinah backed away from the door slowly and ran as fast as she could toward the palace gates.

♥

Six months had passed since that dark night, and Rinton and Thatch, Heart Cards in the king's service, would—when bribed over wine—tell the tale about that evening. The evening when Dinah, the future Queen of Hearts, was found outside the palace walls, dressed only in a lady's slip. She had no recollection of how she got there, no answers for how she escaped through the palace gates without being seen. She was in shock, shivering and deeply afraid. It was the night, they recalled, that the king had introduced the lovely Vittiore, and pondered whether it was a coincidence that it was the same night that Dinah, Princess of Wonderland, proved to be a little mad—just like her brother.

Three

Winter in Wonderland was Dinah's favorite time of year, aside from her father's yearly departure for the Western Slope. Pink snowflakes circled down from a gloomy gray sky as Dinah walked quietly across the snow-covered court-yard. Her fur boots left behind huge footprints as the wind blew tiny swirls of the rosy snow around her ankles. Dinah blew out a breath of cold air and watched it freeze in front of her and fall to the ground with a soft tinkle. A seventeen-year-old shouldn't find such simple things amusing, she told herself, but then she did it again with joy.

Two Heart Cards bowed low as she walked past them, but she saw the mocking smiles that played across their faces. She didn't care—not today. Her black wool cape snapped in the wind as it billowed out behind her. The scent of horses entered her nostrils, and she began to hum happily.

The circular Wonderland stables lay between the iron walls and the palace, on the southwest side, housing every kind of steed imaginable. Despite the stable being immaculately clean, you could smell the manure and wood shavings upon approach. Out from a large, reinforced, center hub stall circled more stalls with spokelike channels between them. Horse after horse slept, ate, and trained in the labyrinthine maze of stalls, indoor riding rings, and tack rooms filled with weaponry and gear. It was designed to keep horses from escaping, and the maze provided a deterrent to those who would attempt to steal any of its pampered inhabitants. Dinah sniffed the frosty air again as she made her way through the maze of stalls. Men, hay, and horses—her favorite smells, because they reminded her of *him*. At the core of the wheel, there was a palpable change in the air. This stall was unlike all the others, with three-foot-thick wooden doors towering over Dinah's head.

She looked up with a shudder as she passed and saw the three Hornhooves staring at her, their apple-sized eyes filled with a thirst for death. She kept her head down and stepped as quietly as she dared. The Hornhooves scared her; they scared everyone. More creatures from hellish depths than horses, Hornhooves stood head and shoulders above the other steeds, the height of two horses combined, with leg muscles thicker than a man's head. Their deadly hooves were covered with hundreds of spiked bones, each one unbreakable: instruments of a painful death for anyone who stood in their way. They were the king's pride and joy, especially Morte. Morte—the bringer of death.

It was Morte who stared down at Dinah now as she passed, steam hot enough to burn skin hissing out of his nostrils. Generous muscles danced under his shimmering black hide—so black it was almost blue. He was larger than the other two white Hornhooves and was rumored to be a particularly bloodthirsty beast—relentless and crueler than most of his kind. The Yurkei tribe had tamed them for generations, and they were bred to be fearless soldiers—the ultimate war horse, virtually unstoppable and very rare. Many a man had died under their hooves, either torn to pieces on their spiked hooves or crushed by their awesome weight. The beasts were so massive that Dinah's spread hand could be swallowed by one of Morte's cavernous black nostrils.

Morte walked to the end of his stall as she moved past, his heavy hooves shaking the ground beneath him. The Hornhooves made Dinah nervous, and she walked faster toward the stables' outside rim, where the lame and the weak horses were kept, still useful for plowing or load bearing. She clicked her tongue and waited for Speckle to come to the edge of his stall.

As a child, Dinah had named him—her black-and-white spotted gelding—Speckle, for he reminded her of a speckle of rain upon her window. He was a kind and gentle horse. Rarely did he do more than trot happily, eat heartily, and bestow sloppy kisses across Dinah's hand. He gave a joyful whinny upon her approach, and she produced an apple from under her cloak. Speckle snatched it up with a happy neigh, his soft horse lips dancing over her hand.

"Do you think I came just to see you?" she whispered to Speckle, scratching his ear. "Sweet horse." She gave him a friendly pat and headed deeper into the outer ring. *Poor Speckle*, she thought, *he is definitely not the reason I visit the stables this day and every day.* An unsteady blush blotched its way up her pale cheeks. Wardley now spent most of his time training the horses and the Cards; therefore, Dinah was spending more and more time with the horses as well.

Wardley Ghane was training to be the next Knave of Hearts—a fancy title for the commander of the Heart Cards, but to Dinah, he was so much more than that. Tall, with long brown curls that brushed the top of his bold eyebrows, Wardley Ghane was as devastatingly handsome as he was skilled. He rode his ebony saddle as if he had been born atop a horse, and he could pull a blade from his belt with the greatest of ease. He was a fearsome warrior, a proud bearer of the king's coat of arms, and a deft Card who could navigate the politics and pitfalls that would inevitably come with ruling over the Heart Cards at such a young age. He was being trained by Xavier Juflee, the current Knave of Hearts, who was widely known as the best swordsman in all Wonderland.

Wardley was the king's favorite of all his young Cards, and maybe someday, Dinah hoped, something much more. She longed to make Wardley her husband, which would make him the King of Hearts beside her. The line of succession decreed that when a king and a queen ruled on the throne, they ruled until death, or until they gave up their throne. If a king or queen died while ruling—as Davianna had—then the firstborn child of that union, upon his or her eighteenth year, would rule beside the widowed parent until the child married. At that time, the older king or queen would give up the throne, and the newly married rulers would take the throne together. Gazing at Wardley's face, Dinah longed for the day when her father would step down to her husband. Much to Dinah's surprise, it seemed the day she turned sixteen, Wardley began to make her heart clench in want with each lazy smile, each friendly hug. She looked at him and wanted more of him—she wanted all of him. The change in her demeanor generally bewildered him, so she tried to keep her fawning to a minimum when they were together; but at night she lay in her bed, imagining his lips on hers, the weight of his body pressed against her. His name was always on the tip of her lips, her desire for him unbridled. She loved him and, in a way, always had. He waited for her now, munching on a handful of berries in the shadow of the palace, already mounted on his dazzling white steed when Dinah emerged from the stalls.

He deftly adjusted his cloak and armor, as he was already suited up for his training with the Cards. On the breast of his white uniform sat a red square with a black heart upon it, the king's blazon. Corning, his blindingly white horse, gave a slight buck as Dinah's black cloak leaped in the winter wind.

"Whooaa there." Wardley tugged his red reins before smiling down at Dinah. "He sees you almost every day, and yet that black cloak always makes him jumpy." He reached down and patted Dinah's braid. "You look nice today!"

She felt a heat rush through her body, warming her to the tips of her toes.

"What are you doing out here on this freezing morning?"

Dinah gave a shrug. "It's not that cold. You've never

been a winter person. I like winter. Here, I brought you warm tarts."

Dinah removed the steaming pastries from the folds of her cloak. The raspberry jam had already leaked through the cheesecloth, and its scent filled the yard.

Wardley licked his lips. "Oh, Dinah, you are too good. This is just what I needed. You're incredible, you know that?" He took the pastry from her hand and shoved it eagerly into his mouth in one terribly messy bite. Powdered sugar dusted his top lip. Dinah smiled shyly as she circled a pink heart in the snow with her boot. Seeing Wardley was sometimes the only happy part of her entire day.

"My father came to see me this morning."

"And he was horrible to you, as always?" As Wardley spoke, puffs of tart flew out of his mouth and floated down onto Corning. Dinah gave Wardley an amused smile.

"Must you always eat as if you were starving?" She pulled a handkerchief from her sleeve and handed it up to him.

He wiped his mouth and smiled. "Sorry. If you must know, I *am* always starving."

"You know my father—he would have to speak to me to be horrible. He came in, had some angry words with Harris, and stormed out, but not before he threw my tray of food on the floor."

Wardley stopped eating and narrowed his eyes. "And then you gave the tarts to me?"

Dinah smiled, her white teeth gleaming against the pink snow. "No. Those are fresh from the kitchen. I threw away the food—well, rather, Emily did."

That was the short version of the story. Really, Dinah cowered in a corner while her father shouted at Harris all the things that Dinah was doing wrong and the depth of his disappointment in her. She wasn't pretty, she was stupid, she wasn't a lady, she wasted her time daydreaming and exploring the castle, she was horrible at croquet, she was unfit to rule. . . . As the king struck Harris with his huge open hand, Dinah withered onto the floor. When the king turned on her, she covered her face and spun away. Her father left with a disgusted sneer. His rages came more and more frequently now, it seemed. When she was a child, he had always been cold and distant, but begrudgingly polite. Now, he openly hated her in front of her servants. The King of Hearts was still cordial in public, but his seething loathing was like a black undercurrent, sucking the color out of every party and public gathering of the royal family. Dinah avoided him at all costs, and even Harris and Emily had learned to stay far away from the King of Hearts and his fiery temper.

Back in the stables, Dinah sat down on an overturned bucket with a huff. "I hate him. He's terrible."

Wardley dismounted his horse with one smooth kick of his leg and wrapped his free arm around Dinah, the other holding fast to his practice sword. "I know your father isn't a great father all the time."

"Or ever," replied Dinah sullenly. "He's not the way a father is supposed to be. He's not anything like your father."

Wardley gave an understanding smile. Unlike Dinah, he adored his gentle father. "I know. But the king must love you; I'm sure he does . . . in his own horrible way. Ruling Wonderland isn't for the fainthearted, and the crown weighs heavy, you know that. You are his daughter, his only viable heir, and someday he will see you for the . . ." He seemed at a loss for words. He patted her cheek lightly, and Dinah stopped breathing. "For the fierce woman that you will become. The Queen of Hearts. A good and just queen, and a doting sister. I see you growing stronger each day, and someday he will see that."

"Someday," she grumbled, "is not today."

Wardley raised his hand, brushing the side of Dinah's cheeks. "You . . ." His voice caught in his throat. "Will be an amazing queen one day."

His touch was like fire on her skin, and she felt her pulse, along with every inch of her, raise to meet his fingers. Her breathing labored as he gently stroked her cheek. She looked up at him expectantly and when their eyes met, Wardley blushed and looked away. He leaped back from her as if she was dangerous, clumsily drawing his sword.

"Then you should tell your father how you feel. Today! I command it."

It took a moment for Dinah to breathe again, but she did, grabbing a broom handle leaning against the stable door and shaking off her black cloak. She took a fighting stance and swung her broomstick at Wardley. He parried and moved to the side.

"I will! I'll tell him, 'Father! You are getting slow and mean in your old age. You are no longer the warrior you once were. Give me my kingdom already, you beast! Then I will defeat the Yurkei, once and for all!'"

Their swords rang together, wood on steel, through the stables and out into the yard. It was a complicated and perfected dance, one they had done thousands of times before. Wardley spun and easily deflected her downswing as Dinah caught him lightly on the hip with the side of the broom handle.

"Ow! That was hard!" He laughed.

He was distracted momentarily, and Dinah swung hard for his head. Wardley ducked and easily lopped off the top of her broom handle with his sword.

"You always go for the head. Always with these ill-planned swings," he lectured. "It leaves you open. Wait for the *right* opportunity, and then go for the strike. Don't go for it the minute you have any opening. You're too impulsive. Xavier has been working with me on identifying my weaknesses, and that, my friend, is yours. It will be the last thing you do in a battle."

Dinah smiled and brushed a string of black hair out of her eyes. "I'll never be in battle. Croquet is the closest I'll come to that, I imagine."

"A queen should know how to defend herself," Wardley answered, picking up the broom piece from the stable floor. "Even if all you do is listen to complaints and grow fat eating warm tarts on your throne. The King of Hearts is a seasoned warrior. He might not be a great father, but I know him as a commander. He is every bit the unyielding man Wonderlanders say he is. You shouldn't be so hard on him. You should hope to be like him in that matter."

"I'm hard on him?" Dinah flung her broken stick away. "I'm hard on *him*? He looks at me only with disgust and contempt. He treats Harris awfully, and gods know what women he has up in the mistresses' chamber every night. . . ."

Wardley pushed his sword into the dirt and grabbed Dinah's arm. It gave a passionate tremor under his calloused skin. "Dinah, *be quiet*." He gave her a gentle shake. "You could be put in the Black Towers for saying such things. I know you haven't had the best time without your mother, but this obvious hatred for your father could get you or, even worse, *me* killed." He gave her a naughty grin, followed by a wink.

The thought stopped the argument rising in Dinah's throat. She would never do anything to hurt Wardley. Never. Wardley had been her constant companion and playmate ever since she could toddle around the castle on chubby legs. When they were younger, Harris and Emily left her frequently with Wardley's mother, a lady of the court, and the two children would scamper off chasing birds and pudgy hedgehogs that roamed the palace grounds. Wardley taught her how to wield a sword, how to ride Speckle, how to pee outside, and how to eat a tart without her hands. To a child, Wonderland Palace was truly full of marvel, and exploring its secrets together had brought Dinah more joy than any other part of her childhood. Wardley was hers and hers alone, something her father could never take from her. Not that it mattered much. The King of Hearts doted on Wardley and encouraged his fine abilities. He tolerated their friendship and almost encouraged it by his lack of anger toward Dinah when Wardley was around. If only she could be near him always. . . .

Dinah turned that last wish in her heart as she scowled at him. "I'm leaving," she snapped. "I don't need to be told what to do by a boy with sugar powder all over his face."

Wardley grinned. "Dinah, c'mon. . . ."

"NO."

She pulled her cloak over her pale-gray dress lined with red hearts and tucked her long black braid back into the hood. "That's the last tart you will ever get from me. Who are you to lecture the Princess of Wonderland? No one, a lowly stable boy."

Wardley pushed his hair back from his forehead and gave her a knowing smile. "All right, but I'll still be hungry tomorrow."

"Good-bye."

"Dinah, wait!"

Her heart throbbed in her chest as she turned back to him. He leaned against the side of Corning, his face close to hers, whispering, "You can't say anything like that about your father again, unless we are outside the palace or in our box in the Heart Chapel, do you understand? I'm serious."

Dinah saw a rare glimpse of fear in his chocolate-brown

eyes. She gave a sigh. "I won't. I won't say anything to get you in trouble, I promise."

"Good." Wardley gave her shoulder a friendly squeeze. "I enjoy having my head." He pulled Corning over by his red reins and mounted up. "Will you come see me again tomorrow, after training?"

"Perhaps. If I have time. I probably won't. Tomorrow is the Royal Croquet Game."

"Ah yes, your favorite day of the year."

Dinah grimaced. She hated the Royal Croquet Game. "Perhaps I can find a way to hit Vittiore with my mallet."

"Go easy on her. I think your father scares her. She seems terrified all the time."

"He should scare her. She's a bastard child, unworthy of a minute of his time. I hope she dies of wheezing fever."

Wardley looked off into the distance, focused on something Dinah couldn't see. "You don't mean that. So, you'll visit me tomorrow, maybe after croquet? Or I'll see you at the game."

Of course, of course, her heart sang, *I will see you every day!* She gave a shrug.

"Good. Before I forget, I have something for Charles. Can you give this to him?" He handed Dinah a tiny wooden seahorse. He had whittled it himself; there was truly nothing Wardley couldn't master.

She turned it over in her hand, admiring his craftsmanship. "He'll love it."

Wardley wheeled Corning around and out into the winter air. "See you tomorrow!" he declared. She smiled and waved as he joined the ranks of Heart Cards, marching in silent formation toward the courtyard, their steps echoing in harsh, single notes. Xavier Juflee patted him hard on the back as they galloped to the front of the line.

Dinah tiptoed out of the stable area, back into the circular labyrinth. As she rounded the endless curves and switchbacks of stalls, she allowed a smile to play across her face. One year ago, in the bright Wonderland sun, Wardley had given Dinah her first kiss, a light brush of his lips over her top one. They had been under the Julla Tree, a massive red skeleton with silky mulberry leaves and buzzing black fruit that opened and closed every hour. As children, they had climbed the Julla Tree hundreds of times, to play Tribes and Cards or to spy on the ladies' bathing quarters. Now, they escaped to the leafy shelter to have a minute of stillness with each other—Wardley from his endless training, and Dinah from her lessons and, sometimes, her father.

It had been summer then, and Dinah was sixteen years old. The lunch trumpets had sounded from the Royal Apartments, and Dinah had reluctantly dropped the fruit she had been snacking on and slipped down the tree. Her ankle twisted at the bottom, and she fell, cutting her leg open on the tree's thorny roots—fat fingers that twisted up from the ground to protect the tree. Wardley followed her and gently wiped the blood from her leg with his hand.

"Are you okay?" he'd asked, holding her leg in his large hand. Dinah gave him a brave smile, though she felt like sobbing. She didn't want Wardley to see her cry, even though he had several times—like when Vittiore had a costume ball thrown in her honor, when Harris began teaching Vittiore in the evenings instead of Dinah, or when her father had forgotten to send her tea on All Tea's Day.

Wardley wiped his hand on the Julla Tree's fuzzy trunk, looked deeply into her black eyes, and kissed her. His lips were cool and soft, and his mouth tasted like lemons. Dinah leaned in, but he had pulled back, resting his hands on her flaming cheeks, his eyes filled with curiosity as he took in her face. He was trying to understand something; she could see it in his eyes. Dinah gasped, purely out of shock at the sudden heat rushing through her veins, and Wardley gave an easy shrug. "Just wanted to see what it felt like." He swung himself back into the Julla Tree with a laugh, and Dinah walked, dazed and giddy, toward the castle.

A year had passed since then, and Dinah could still feel the touch of his lips upon hers as she wound her way out of the stables. Layers of pink snow dusted the swirling gold spires of Wonderland Palace, and the entire kingdom seemed to hold its breath with a still glow. A large group of Spade Cards was lounging near the red-glass doors that led into the palace. Dinah pulled her cloak over her head, hoping to hide her face, but her lips gave an uncertain jerk as she moved closer to them. They stood with an exaggerated ease, snickers escaping their blackened mouths.

"Your HIGH-ness." They gave slight bows.

As she passed, she heard one of them murmuring under

his breath: "The king's daughter, disgrace to the throne. Looks nothing like her mother."

"Recard," whispered another.

Dinah's heart was flapping wildly now. An uncontrollable rage started at her fingertips and worked its way into her chest. She stumbled, and the tiny wooden seahorse that Wardley had given her dropped from her hand. It rolled to a rest against the steel-tipped boot of a Spade.

"Aye, what's this?" He bent down and picked it up, the figure minuscule against his large hand. "A toy? Aren't yeh a bit old for toys, Princess?"

"It's a seahorse, and it's *mine*. Please give it back." Dinah raised her eyes to meet his, hoping her trembling lip wouldn't betray the shame she felt. "Please."

The Spade gave Dinah a hard look. "Come and get it, Yer Highness."

His eyes were a mottled gold, she noted with surprise. It was such a stark color against his black-on-black uniform, his long gray hair, and the black symbol of a spade tattooed underneath his right eye. The other Spades remained motionless, half-bowed, as Dinah took a timid step toward him. She started to extend her left hand for the seahorse and then thought better of it. *I am the Princess of Wonderland*, she told herself. *Remember what Harris says. Someday I will be queen.*

"No."

The Spades jerked their heads up with curiosity.

"I am the Princess of Wonderland, and you will put it in my hand."

The gold-eyed Spade gave a deep hoot. "Aye, indeed you are, although the other princess has the look of one. If it were up to me, pretty Lady Vittiore would be the one getting the crown."

Rising anger burned her spine. With a swift movement, Dinah reached up and struck the Spade, hard across his face. One of her pearl rings left a thin trail of blood across his left cheek. He lunged at her, only to catch himself, his fist inches from her face. Dinah reveled in his shock.

"The Lady Vittiore is not a princess, she is only a duchess. Now, you will put the toy in my hand."

The Spade gave her an amused smile. "No problem, Princess." He reached out.

"No. My other hand."

He looked down with a grimace at her other arm, tucked firmly within her cloak. She made no move to pull it out for him. The other Spades watched in shock as he tried in vain to get the seahorse into her hand without groping her, an action surely punishable by death. Dinah watched the farce silently, as if her arm were detached from her body and she was merely a spectator to this man fumbling around her cloak. Finally, the ashamed Spade pressed the toy into her palm, and Dinah closed her fist around it. The Spade walked back to the barrel he had been sitting on and leaned over it, peering at Dinah. A keen interest now replaced what had been mockery on his face moments earlier.

"Eh, so yeh have some of your father's fiery blood in you then, do you?"

Dinah scowled at him. "Speak to me again and I'll have you sent to the Black Towers in a coffin. What is your name?"

The man paled. "I was just joking, Yer Highness. Please don't report me to the king."

"I said, *What is your name?*"

His dirty hands wrung together. "Gorrann. Sir Gorrann."

"Well, Sir Gorrann, I will not report you to the king this day. But if you ever insult me again, I will have your head. No need to involve the king."

With a hard look she brushed past them, her black cloak trailing behind her. As soon as the red-glass palace doors closed behind her, Dinah plunged into an empty corridor off the main hall. Her lips parted in a soft cry, but she steeled herself from the shame. Victorious, she clutched the wooden seahorse in one sweaty hand and wiped the tears from her face with the other as she made her way to her brother's chambers.

Four

Charles's quarters were located in the western tower of the Royal Apartments, situated neatly above the castle's kitchens. Her father had given in building materials what he never gave Charles in life. The king showed no other sign of love, affection, or even duty to his son. Charles's room, as a result, was one of the strangest places in the entire palace. Huge white columns inlaid with red hearts twisted up to the ceiling where they met an expansive fresco featuring all the creatures of Wonderland. Hornhooves, gryphons, birds of all types, great whales, white-striped bears, and four-winged dragons danced across the ceiling in rich paints.

It would have been lovely—a gorgeous work of art—if crudely drawn hats had not been scribbled across the creatures in black charcoal. The animals now wore ugly slashes of feathers, top hats, and huge fedoras in wavy, messy lines that ran from one to another without stopping. The hats were richly detailed, the lines between them angry slashes—the art of madness.

Sad, Dinah thought as she gazed upward, her hood falling back onto her neck, *that madness and genius were always melded together in this room.*

The room itself was a testament to Charles's obsession. Racks upon racks of hats rose up from the floor, twisting and circling between rickety, half-built staircases that led to nothing but air. Doors had been attached to the hat racks, swinging open and shut with the cold air blowing in from a large open window at the top of the main staircase. This staircase was Charles's favorite, covered with hundreds of bolts and swatches of fabric. Piles of melting snow were accumulating on the window ledge in little drifts. Dinah gave a sigh and climbed up one of the rickety staircases, shutting the window firmly and securing the clasp. She heard a skittering of tiny feet below.

"Charles. You cannot leave the window open when it's snowing outside. It's bitterly cold in here, and the snow will get all over your new hats. We've talked about this." She dusted off a sturdy gray fedora with orange canary feathers embroidered into a sun and stars. "You have to be careful with them."

At her feet, a matted head of dirty yellow hair rose up in a space between the wide stair treads. "Pink snow on pink hats makes the walrus dance. He dances on the sea, hee-hee!"

Charles jumped out from under the staircase. Dinah gasped as he fell to the floor, somersaulting on his rough landing and leaping up into a kicking dance. "Snow on the hat, snow on the hat, black like your Cheshire Cat!"

He gave a high-pitched giggle, and Dinah laughed with him. Charles was younger by only two years, but in his madness he was practically ageless. He was a genius, a savant, a helpless infant and naughty child, all mixed into one tiny boy. He had been born mad—a squealing infant who never slept, a silent toddler who would bang his head against the wall, a curious boy who once ate glass and loved nothing more than to look at the stars. Davianna, Dinah's mother, had loved her crazed son fiercely and was best at dealing with him. When she curled her arms around him, clutching him to her chest as though she could squeeze the madness out, he relaxed and was content, even as he babbled nonsensically. With his mother's intense love and focus, Charles seemed to be improving, step by tiny step. When she died, he went completely maniacal and never returned.

He was regularly found wandering around the castle, a dead bird in one hand and a tart in the other. It was as likely that he had taken a bite out of one as he had the other. He once walked off the Great Hall balcony, breaking both legs on the marble steps below. After that, his walk consisted of short steps and a trotting leap—the grotesque gait of the permanently insane.

Then he stopped eating for a while. Not even Dinah, his beloved sister, could get him to eat. Barely more than a child herself at ten years old, she pleaded with him as she tried to shove a tart, soup, quail, anything into his open mouth. He grew weaker, retreating completely into his own wondrous world, and the entire kingdom dressed in black, awaiting the death of the little Prince of Hearts.

On what surely could have been one of his final nights, Dinah brought in a trunk full of their deceased mother's clothing. She tucked it all around him, her dresses, slips, and socks, so that he might be comforted on his journey to another place. Charles's fingers had found one of her mother's bejeweled hats, the one she had worn for All Tea's Day the year before—a gorgeous plum hat with a tall plume, plump and glittering in his small hand. An absurd smile played across his translucent skin as he turned the hat over and over in his hands, a look of fascination on his face. He then turned to Dinah and simply asked for a biscuit.

"My Dinah," he had whispered with a smile, his small hand tracing her chin. "Biscuit?"

She saw it in his eyes that day—he had decided to stay, just like that. That was seven years ago. Since then, Charles never left his room. He watched the world from his windows, where he occasionally threw his lavishly made hats down onto adoring townspeople. A hat created by Charles, the so-called Mad Hatter, was worth more than any piece of clothing in Wonderland. His creations were inspired works of skill and insanity. Unapologetically whimsical, rich in every color found in nature and some that weren't, they were a testament to Charles's lunacy.

He rarely slept or bathed. His two loyal servants, Lucy and Quintrell, saw to all his needs. They kept his chambers from falling into disrepair but allowed his mind the freedom to create in the wild lunacy that he fostered. Tapestries and huge rolls of fabric covered the ground and most of the walls. Narrow walkways had been created for the servants, but Charles simply danced over the rainbow floor, his feet barely brushing the patterned fabrics of amethyst, pumpkin, taupe, and lapis.

Charles looked up at Dinah, still standing on the stairway. He giggled and sang, "A ribbon across their necks, one, two, hearts. Check and check!"

She looked down at the tawny head and the mismatched blue and green eyes that stared back at her wildly. "Do you remember my name today?"

"Dinah, rhymes with lima, beans and more beans,

growing up and up, over the hills into the pale white, like sugar on a pie, die, die . . ."

Dinah gave him a proud smile. "That's right, Charles. Dinah. Your sister. I brought you something today."

His right eye blinked twice. "Something? Something like the sun, inching closer every day. It will burn us, uh-oh, it will."

"Not quite the sun, but something really special." Dinah reached into her cloak and pulled out the tiny wooden seahorse. Charles's eyes widened, and he took it in his slight, feminine hands. Wardley had carved swirls into its curving back and blackened its long nose with smudged charcoal.

"It's from Wardley. Remember him? What do you say?"

Charles repaid Dinah with a huge smile that showed his misshapen teeth. "Blue horse, swimming on a long field. Tasty shrimp inside his ribs, I can taste it, yes I can!"

"I'm glad you like it."

Charles held the carving up into the light as he made it swim through the air. "Sea birds, shimmering scales, black eyes . . ."

He dashed away from her and began riffling through

the fabrics, muttering to himself. Dinah had seen this a hundred times before. The inspiration for a hat had taken root in his mangled brain—a creative, aggressive root that was spreading its joy and poison through each and every secret path of his mind. Dinah descended the staircase to speak with the servants who were waiting patiently near the door.

"How is he doing this week?" she asked.

Lucy gave a deep bow. She was the gentlest woman Dinah had ever known, a grandmother of three with rosy cheeks and white hair that glowed a pale blue in the harsh winter light. Age lines rippled out from her eyes and down her neck into her modest white gown. On her head sat an enormous felt whale, embroidered with swirling pink blossoms. Charles loved her dearly, in his own way, and Lucy was his most devoted servant.

Quintrell was her assistant—a strapping lad who handled the physical labor involved with Charles's care. He wrestled Charles into the swan-shaped tub once a week and scrubbed him down with hedgehog skins while the boy screamed and writhed. He was also the only one who could force Charles to eat when he was in one of his hat-making furies. Charles periodically went through long periods where he saw nothing but fabric and stitching—fits of wild, brilliant mania that would last for days. Dinah had no idea how Lucy and Quintrell dealt with Charles day in and day out, but they seemed content. Other than Dinah, they were the only ones who truly loved him.

Though he was her brother, Dinah felt that she floated in a strange emotional fog with Charles—she loved him dearly, but her love was always tinged with confusion. She couldn't deal with him the way Lucy and Quintrell did. Charles recognized her most weeks, but when he didn't, Dinah felt betrayed, even more alone than usual. Dinah watched as Lucy wrinkled her face, sorting a pile of buttons into several different boxes. She cleared her throat, preparing to respond to Dinah's question. "How is he doing, Your Highness? Well, he has created two hats in the last twenty days, which is fast for him—the fuchsia beret with swallow's eggs, and the gryphon top hat, which will be delivered to Lord and Lady Clutessa next week. Both works were inspired by the birds that have nested just outside the window."

Dinah nodded. Working for Charles had turned both

Lucy and Quintrell into hatters as well—they were as skilled and knowledgeable as any milliner in town could ever be.

"They sound beautiful. But I was asking about Charles. Has he been well?" Quintrell fidgeted nervously. Dinah smiled. "Well, out with it."

"Your Highness, three nights past, I woke up to loud giggling coming from the atrium." Quintrell glanced nervously at Lucy. She placed her withered hand on his arm and nodded for him to continue. "When I came out into the room, Charles was up on one of the staircases. He . . ." Quintrell's voice caught in his throat.

Lucy stepped forward. "Charles had one of the stitching needles dug into his arm. He was squeezing the blood out and letting it drip onto the mulberry silk."

A painful gasp escaped from Dinah's lips. "Why, why would he *do* that?"

Lucy refused to meet her eyes. "He said the dye wasn't the right shade of red. He was *fixing* it. We tried to get the needle away from him, but he was on the edge of the staircase, so . . ."

"So you let him do it, rather than risk his falling."

They both nodded. Dinah was tempted to rage at them the way she had raged at the Spade, but it was no use. She knew Charles, and she knew that he couldn't be controlled, bottled, or taught. His mind worked in a different way—short flashes of brilliance followed by dark plunges into his macabre imaginary world.

"Did you take away all his sewing needles?"

"Yes, Your Highness. We only let him use the small needles now, which have actually led to the production of some very detailed, elaborate work."

Dinah looked over at Charles, who was gleefully slashing apple-green taffeta into thin ribbons with his long fingernails. She climbed up the stairs and kissed him on the side of the head. His dirty hair, ever matted and wild, always smelled a bit like her mother.

"I have to go now, but I'll be back in a few days," she told him.

Charles whipped his head around to stare at animals on the ceiling and began singing. "Days and nights, the king sings. Tusks and musks and wooble fire. He sings with a black tongue, fire in his lungs, his lungs."

"Where did the seahorse go?" Dinah asked.

Charles opened his mouth, stuck out his tongue, and stroked it slowly. "Down, down, down the rabbit hole!" he crowed.

Dinah shut her eyes.

"Not to worry, Your Highness. We'll find it," Lucy promised, before she returned to sorting buttons.

Charles was still singing when Dinah walked out of the atrium, her heart compressing with each step. The song, so lovely and mad, followed her down the marble hallways as she walked back to her chambers.

Lying in front of her door was an elaborately folded invitation—her summons to the Royal Croquet Game. It had already been opened, the seal of the king broken. With a sigh, she untied the seven pink ribbons that held the card in place. Something was leaking through the envelope—ink? Dinah pulled the card out and tilted the elaborate calligraphy into the light.

Your presence for the Royal Croquet Game is requested. The Princess of Wonderland will play in the final game against her opponents, the Duchess of Wonderland and the King of Hearts.

Dinah felt the air whoosh out of her lungs. She had never played against her father before, ever. She was always set against a lady of the court—someone she could easily beat—and the king was always paired with Xavier Juflee, the Knave of Hearts.

The black liquid dripped again, this time landing on her shoe. Dinah turned the envelope upside down with a shake.

The head of a white mouse, severed at the neck, fell out of the envelope and bounced on the floor. Dinah leaped back with a shriek. Shaking, she turned the invitation over, but there was nothing on it. Kneeling, she touched the mouse head with the end of a trembling finger. A new feeling shot through her, and she felt her senses heighten as she stared at the tiny lips of the mouse, pulled back in a macabre smile. Dinah was both fascinated and afraid, devastated that there was even more reason to dread tomorrow.

Five

Dinah spooned plum pudding over her flat fig biscuits as Harris hopped back and forth in front of her, wine dashing out from his large goblet. "You are going to be late, late, late for the Royal Croquet Game. We cannot be late, Your Highness." Harris shuffled around the table, his long checkered robe flapping after him.

"I would rather get run over by Hornhooves than play croquet with Vittiore today," grumbled Dinah, draining a glass of juice. The mouse head still weighed heavily on her mind, and she couldn't shake the image of it bouncing across the stone floor.

"That may be the case, Princess, but you still must go. It is the precursor to All Tea's Day, and it is expected of the royal family to not only be in attendance, but also to play after all the townspeople have finished their games. This tradition goes back hundreds and hundreds of years . . ."

Dinah gave a groan and interrupted Harris's rambling. "Starting with the seventh King of Hearts, Doylan the Great, the Royal Croquet Game has established the game's rules and etiquette. It has made the Royal Family of Hearts synonymous with croquet, forever entwined in its grand traditions and all it stands for," Dinah said, and smiled coyly. "You give me the same speech every year. I remember. Contrary to what you believe, I listen to you. Now, may I please read in peace?"

One of her history texts, *The Great Crane*, sat open in front of her, a large silver book with worn pages. It was a rare book, and a fascinating fictional history of the Yurkei religion. Harris flung wide the doors to the courtyard, letting a swirl of pink snow into the room.

"Please close that. I'm freezing," mumbled Dinah.

The old man ignored her. "Croquet!" he boomed. "The very name conjures a vision of Wonderland excellence, aristocracy, and grace."

Dinah let out a sigh, gently shut her book, and balanced her face on the palms of her hands.

"The Royal Croquet Game sets the tone of the next year's fashion, manners, teas, and style. It is an opportunity for the Royal Family of Hearts to show their unity, their athletic prowess . . ."

Dinah's head jerked up with her laugh, a smudge of plum pudding across her upper lip. "Athletic prowess? Harris, we are hitting balls with sticks. Unity? My father hates me, and Vittiore—"

"Is a lovely, innocent girl," finished Harris.

Dinah shot him a nasty look. "Is a venomous wench snake," she replied. "The very sight of her makes me ill. She may be my sister by my father's unfaithful blood, but she is *not* my sibling. Only Charles is my true sibling. Who, may I remind you, is never invited to the Royal Croquet Game!"

Harris adjusted his spectacles. "Dinah, you know very

well why Charles is never invited."

"Because he's an embarrassment to my father?"

"Because he cannot be controlled, and the Line of Hearts must appear strong and unbroken. The history of the Royal Croquet Game is filled with political pandering and glorious grandeur, and it's no place for someone who is mad."

Dinah brought her knife down through the biscuits on the table.

"He may be mad, but he is my *brother*. And he's the son of the king. If he wasn't mad, he would be the rightful heir of Wonderland and every Card would bow before him."

Harris reached down and wiped Dinah's lip with his white handkerchief, a tiny heart embroidered on the corner. "That is certainly true, Princess. No one grieves the loss of the prince's mind more than I do. I was there when he was born, as I was with you. I held his red, squirming body in my hands, wrapped him up in fur, and blessed him in the name of the Wonderland gods. I love Charles, but even I know that he cannot be included in royal events. He makes the crown look weak, and it draws attention to the fractures in your family."

Dinah stabbed her plate angrily. "When I am queen, Charles will not be hidden away in some grand atrium, throwing hats out of windows. He will join me where I go, mad or not."

Harris pulled the chair out from under her, and Dinah jumped to her feet. "That is my greatest wish, Princess. Now, it is time to get dressed! We are late! Emily, bring her croquet gowns!"

There were few things as awful, Dinah mused, as being strapped into a corset as if she were being bound to her own torso. She stood, arms outstretched, as Emily dressed her. Emily was grunting as Dinah's strong ribs and square hips shrank gradually into a curvy, maidenly form, made perfect by thick ribbons.

As the pressure slowly increased, Dinah studied herself in a long, heart-shaped mirror. Shiny black hair fell straight from her temple to shoulders. The hair was incredibly thick and heavy, a burden that Dinah could barely tolerate some days. Her face was soft cream, made even dewier by her deep red lips. They formed a perfect pout—a little heart on a strong face. Her black-brown eyes were huge and fringed with long lashes—arguably her best asset. *Yes, strong*, she thought, twisting her body around. *Strong like my father and dark like my mother.*

Dinah was a bit leaner than the average Wonderland woman. She had firm, square shoulders, like a man. Her middle was solid, her legs squat. There was no curve from her bust to her waist—she was one solid square, topped with an ample bosom, more small melons than the ripe peaches described in Emily's tawdry novels. Tarts had added a bit of softness to her chin as of late, but Dinah was still attractive, or at least that's what she told herself. Not pretty or delicate like Vittiore, but perhaps handsome.

A Card had once called her handsome, and Dinah had cried for days, but now she could see it. Her mother had been broad but voluptuous, and for this reason her hourglass figure still graced many a painting. Her long black hair had reached the ground, and she carried her crown with great ease and beauty. Davianna had been so elegant in gowns and crowns, whereas Dinah always felt more like one of the ridiculous birds that Charles so frequently pinned onto hats.

"You cannot make my waist any smaller without killing me," she snapped at Emily.

Emily laid her slipper against Dinah's back to brace herself and gave a final tug. The bone ribbing ripped into Dinah's side, and she let out a gasp of pain.

"There," said Emily, with a self-satisfied smile. "Now I'm done, Your Highness."

She fetched Dinah's gown and draped it carefully over her head. The thick gray wool fell around Dinah like a curtain, hanging heavily over every inch of her. The gown was lovely in a severe way, with hundreds of gray fabrics mingling together in an elaborate tweed. A large red heart arched over her shoulders and down the back of the dress, its top folds meeting at her collarbone. White ribbons ran up and down the heart in delicate ruffles. Bright raspberry hearts dotted the full hem of the dress.

Emily buttoned the dress up the back and began working on Dinah's hair. She swept it away from Dinah's face, twisting and twisting until a voluminous bun decorated the back of her head. Long, silver heart pins were stuck into the bun, which was then covered with a red, jeweled hair net.

Harris came over, carrying a crystal box.

"No," said Dinah. "No, no, no."

Harris ignored her and opened the box, pulling out a long purple brush. With a smile, he began brushing a thin, white powder over her face with the long-handled bristle brush. Dinah sneezed, and they were enveloped in a dusty cloud.

"A princess should *not* struggle so," reprimanded Harris. "You should be thrilled to be a part of this honorable tradition. What a gift it would be to play on the Royal Court." He stepped back with a sigh and summoned Emily to his side. "Bring the crown."

Emily slowly settled Dinah's thin crown onto her head. The unbroken line of red ruby hearts shimmered like fire upon her dark hair and powdered white skin. Harris gave a deep bow, though Dinah saw his legs quake with the effort. He was growing older, and it saddened her so.

"My future queen. You are so beautiful. It brings me such pride to see you as a woman."

Dinah caught his hand and pulled him up, taking in his kind round face. "My dearest friend. Someday I will be queen and you will never have to bow again. You will spend your days eating tarts and leaning on pillows while other servants see to your every need."

Harris gave a sly smile. "Your reign will be wonderful, I'm sure, but I would hope that Your Highness could find better uses for me than lounging on pillows. Perhaps an advisory position on the council."

"Perhaps."

Dinah heard the brassy blare of a single trumpet from outside her balcony. The royal family was being summoned for the game.

The Croquet Lawn was in the very center of the palace yard—a perfectly coiffed square of bright green surrounded by the impassive towers of Wonderland Palace. Looming piles of pink snow had been shoveled into giant mountains that bordered the sides of the green, and the lawn itself looked as lush as it would on a hot summer day instead of the end of winter. Sturdy wooden steps on three sides of the lawn provided ample seating for the hundreds of lords and ladies of the court. On lower wooden stands, thousands of townspeople gazed down on the players. From there they could admire, gossip, and pass judgment on everyone—a favorite pastime during the Royal Croquet Game.

Dinah waited on one side of the lawn, flanked by Harris and twelve Heart Cards who stood at the ready to assist her. The Master of the Games bowed before Dinah and then beckoned her forward. Dinah took a deep breath and murmured a silent prayer that this would be over quickly. Musicians, shoved on top of each other in an elaborately decorated box, raised their long trumpets and blasted out a three-note greeting. Dinah lifted her strong chin and walked out onto the field. There was a polite wave of clapping as she approached the green, her gray dress brushing the sharp blades of grass.

When she got to the middle of the lawn, she looked around with surprise. If she was to play Vittiore she should have been already waiting, in the correct order of hierarchy. Dinah felt a bolt of joy rush through her—perhaps this meant Vittiore would not be joining them! It would be Dinah and her father, playing singles. Her heart gave a weak flutter of hope. Perhaps her father would see that she was a worthy daughter, his strong heir. She would play her best,

Dinah told herself, without any whining or boasting. She would be a picture-perfect vision of the future queen.

The Master of the Games sauntered up and handed Dinah a long wooden mallet shaped like a flamingo, the official palace bird. Dinah liked the heavy weight of the mallet in her palm. These mallets were carved from trees of the Twisted Wood. Crystallized and ancient, these trees took months to chop through, and because of that, only one was able to be felled per year. Its wood was sold at the highest prices in Wonderland proper, fetching a hundredfold more than normal wood. Soldiers wanted it for their sword hilts, farmers for their plows, women for their kitchen spoons. The only part of the tree that wasn't sold was used for the croquet mallets for the royal family.

Dinah waited now, whacking the heavy mallet impatiently against her leg until she heard the trumpets roar for the second time. Biting her lip, Dinah gave an elaborate bow in anticipation of her father. As her eyes surveyed the ground, she heard an intake of breath from the crowd. Her black eyes wandered up, expecting to see her father in all his grandeur, but instead she saw a vision of sweeping beauty. A wave of disappointment passed through her. Vittiore had floated out onto the court. Her long gown was made of several hundred layers of chiffon in creamy, shimmering shades: peach, rose, and lemon all blended together into an exquisite loveliness. Her golden hair had been curled into plump ringlets that cascaded down her back. On her head was a Mad Hatter pillbox hat adorned with white coq feathers. They were attached with a large gemstone the size and color of a peach.

Hot rage boiled up inside of her, and Dinah's mallet dropped from her hand. It was her mother's brooch. Dinah had loved that brooch as a child, often pretending it was an actual peach as she toddled around her mother's bedroom. Vittiore gave Dinah a polite bow and whispered her courtesies. "Your Highness. You look lovely in gray."

Dinah took a menacing step toward Vittiore. "Is that a joke?" she asked through clenched teeth.

Vittiore looked bewildered. "No?"

With one sure step, Dinah thought, *I could plant my ruby slippers into her pretty face.*

"Ah, I see the princess is anxious to begin the game." Cheshire, clothed in dazzling purple, slithered around

Dinah and Vittiore, putting himself between them. "The Royal Croquet Game, Your Highness and Your Grace, must always be played with dignity. I should remind you both that the entire kingdom is watching." While he quietly berated them, his black eyes lingered only on Dinah, who bit down on her lip until she felt a tiny drop of blood on her tongue.

She earnestly smiled up at him. "Of course, Sir Cheshire. One should never conduct oneself with anything other than honesty and charity. A man of virtue like you reminds us of that."

Cheshire stared at her, his eyes darkening with anger, though the wide smile on his face betrayed nothing. Dinah felt a stab of fear. Vittiore gave Dinah an apologetic smile and took her mallet. "We will remember, Sir Cheshire. I have much looked forward to playing with my sister." She raised her pale, slender arms and waved to the crowd, who gave wild roars of approval, followed by shouted marriage proposals. It was the sort of reception that Dinah had never received, not even once.

Cheshire put his thin hand on Dinah's shoulder, squeezed it, and whispered in her ear. "Take comfort in the fact that she is probably quite cold in that thin dress. A queen should be wise above being beautiful."

Then he was gone, back to standing beside her father's Heart Cards, his arms tucked behind his back, his knowing expression resumed. Though she still hated Cheshire and remembered when he had locked her out of the palace, Dinah allowed herself to take comfort in the dimpled goose bumps that ran up Vittiore's arms and bosom. She was indeed snug in her warm gray wool, even if she did look matronly compared to the radiant duchess. She looked to the crowd and spotted Wardley, standing in his Heart Card uniform at the edge of the lawn. He raised his hand in a silent hello, but his face held a mangled frown as he stared at Vittiore. Dinah was relieved that she wasn't the only one to notice this public slight.

Finally, after several trumpet blasts, her father stomped out onto the court, his iron footsteps ricocheting off the marble sidewalk. His wavy blond hair was pushed back from his face by his heavy golden crown, and his cheeks were the ruddy red that comes with drink. Her father hated the Royal Croquet Game as much as she did. He much preferred hunting sports—killing deer or wild horses just outside the castle walls, or tracking down the large sea cats that prowled the Western Slope. He loved the chase, that intense moment when the animals fought for their lives, all for naught, for they were fated to be the royal dinner. The king cleared his throat.

"Give me my mallet!" he bellowed.

His gaze rested on Dinah as he waited. She kept her black eyes glued to the ground, but she could feel the searing heat of his gaze. The three players lined up and were handed a velvet bag containing their wooden balls, carved like hedgehogs. Dinah's were red, the king's black, and Vittiore's white. The Master of Games sauntered to the center of the lawn and explained the rules. A drumroll began as the players walked onto the court. Her father gently took Vittiore's arm and led her to stand next to him. A sharp jealousy swam through Dinah. She shot a pitiful look in Harris's direction. He gave her a kind smile and nervously rubbed the lenses of his glasses with his handkerchief. She raised her head to take in the rapidly shifting clouds, to pretend she was anywhere but here. As the players reached their mark, a single horn blared out a triumphant sound and the crowd gave a roar of applause. Bobbing white lanterns bordering the lawn were lit, and the Royal Croquet Game began.

Vittiore was the first striker. Her opening turn with the mallet sent her white ball hurtling through two wickets, but her second shot didn't get her close to the outside wicket. Dinah was next. She had never been skilled at croquet, despite weekly lessons that she despised. Her red ball went through the first gate but got caught on the second wicket. Her second shot left her ball in her father's way. The King of Hearts took the next turn. His ball sailed through the gates on the first try, whacking Dinah's ball out toward the course boundaries.

Vittiore gave a triumphant giggle. "Excellent hit, Father!"

He took his extra strokes to send his black sphere hurtling toward the third wicket. Vittiore took her second turn, the gentle nudge of her mallet sending her white ball through the obstacle. Dinah got her red ball headed back in the right direction, but she hadn't even taken a single turn before one of her father's black balls was targeting her red ones. Dinah recognized his strategy immediately. Isolate the opponent. Attack with relentless fury. Dominate. Eliminate.

As she watched her father smile encouragingly at Vittiore sending one of her white balls into a bush, Dinah felt the black fury rising inside of her, making the tips of her fingers tingle. Two could play this game, she thought—she wouldn't let herself be humiliated by his misplaced doting. When her turn came again, she swung her mallet hard, unladylike. Her red ball sailed through the wicket, and with a smack, it sent Vittiore's ball completely off the course in a perfect roquet. The crowd gave a murmur of disapproval. *Poor Vittiore.* Dinah didn't care.

Another horn blasted, and the game advanced in complexity once the birds were let loose. A dozen birds ran wild over the course—flamingoes, dodos, pale white swans, and ducks. They got in the way of the balls or blocked stakes or pecked at players' heels. It was chaos. A dodo sank its beak into Vittiore's smooth calf, and she let out a scream, which made Dinah's heart leap with joy. Yet even with the whimsy of the birds and the lighthearted mood of the crowd, both Dinah and her father seemed to sense a turn in the purpose of the game as they attacked each other with relish. Red and black balls cracked against one another continuously as their mallets swung higher and higher. Vittiore was almost forgotten, but just when she would draw close to the eleventh wicket, Dinah would send a red ball her way and she would be pushed backward.

Time seemed to stretch on forever as the three wound their way through hoop after hoop. The crowd grew silent and tense as they sensed the enmity between Dinah and her father. Dark circles of sweat had formed under the king's arms and across Dinah's brow. Her heavy wool dress was swampy inside, and Dinah dreamed of casting it off into the crowd. Her thin ruby crown lay uncomfortably on her head, its sharp points pulling her hair out strand by strand as she bent and twisted, beyond caring how she looked.

After an hour had passed, Cheshire strode out to the middle of the lawn and signaled for the bird catchers. The birds were gathered and removed for the final round, signaling the end of the game. Vittiore had three hoops left and would not win. She forfeited with an easy smile to the crowd and a wave of her hand. They gave a great cheer as she retired, her blond curls untouched by any of the physical strain that Dinah and her father were suffering. Cheshire led her to the edge of the lawn, where she collapsed into a large heart-shaped chair. She was so charming in that self-effacing way: a toss of her hair, a twinkle in her blue eyes. It made Dinah feel dismal and jealous at the same time.

It was Dinah's turn. Her emotions tangled inside of her, and she brought her mallet down with vengeance upon her red ball. It sailed across the lawn with a loud *crack* and slammed into her father's last black ball, which rolled out of bounds and rested against the foot of a mortified Heart Card. He stepped back, and wisely so, for the next sound Dinah heard was her father's rushing cry of rage. He took three steps toward Dinah and violently pulled her close. Both Harris and Cheshire stepped toward the lawn, ready to intervene. The king's huge fingers sank into Dinah's shoulder as a cruel look stretched over his face. To the crowd, it looked like a funny moment between father and daughter. But Dinah could see the enraged indignation in his eyes and could smell the wine as his breath washed over her face.

"Princess, you *will* let me win this game. You will not

humiliate me in front of my kingdom any more than your mere existence already does. The King of Hearts will not lose to his pathetic daughter, or you will find yourself a new mentor, and Harris will find himself suddenly a Spade."

Hot tears welled in Dinah's eyes as he shook her loose. She tried to summon the same boldness that dwelled in her when she had whacked his ball off the lawn, but it was not there. It was replaced by a gnawing hunger for her father's love, so powerful and real that it made her gasp.

"I will," she whispered. "I will do whatever you ask, Father. I'm sorry."

"Do not forget your place again. I am your king and Vittiore is your sister, and you will honor us both. After the game, you will bow before her so all Wonderland can see that you have accepted her as your blood sibling and equal."

A shocked sob escaped from her clenched lips. He smiled and gestured to the crowd. "She takes the game so seriously!" he announced. "My sweet daughter."

He released her. Dinah stepped back, her knees threatening to buckle underneath her. The Master of Games walked to the center of the lawn and spoke into a large silver horn. "The final play of the Royal Croquet Game will now commence. Please stand for your king."

The crowd rose to its feet. The king had the final stroke. He unclasped the four-Card brooches that fastened his cloak and flung it toward Wardley. Wardley scooped it off the field and strode quickly back to his place on the border, but not before he shot Dinah a sympathetic look. The king's ball rolled easily through the last wicket and struck the final stake. All eyes turned to her, including her father's. His face was a distorted tangle of pride and fear, like a bear in a cage. He belonged on a battlefield, not a croquet lawn. Or a throne.

Dinah raised her eyes to take in this macbre scene only to catch Wardley staring at her, his face a mix of admiration and fear. Their eyes met, and he gave Dinah a small, secret smile that warmed her heart. Dinah raised her mallet. There was an intake of breath, and she looked at the crowd, their anxious faces yearning for their king's victory. They feared him without knowing him, worshipped him without any proof of his divinity. She understood at once what it took to be a leader—one had to be willing to be a figurehead without any trace of intimacy. One had to be the projection of even the lowest born's hopes and fears. She understood. This crowd needed her father to win.

She brought the flamingo's beak down hard against her red ball. It sailed across the yard and bounced off the edge of the peg. The crowd erupted into glorious cheering. The king raised his mallet above his head in a sign of victory.

Vittiore rushed to him, her dress floating across the short green grass. "Father! Congratulations."

He swept her up in a warm embrace. Dinah dropped her mallet on the lawn and walked off the green. Harris followed behind her, his head hung in mutual disappointment. Harris had long ago learned to read Dinah's moods and knew when to reprimand . . . and when to stay silent. Dinah walked through the palace quickly, making her way through the twisty stone halls to her bedchamber. She pulled off her gray wool gown, reeking of sour sweat, and fell onto her down mattress. A surge of self-pity washed over her, and she turned her face into the pillow. A soft hand, withered and thin-skinned with time, trailed through her hair. She felt Harris sit beside her.

"I know you missed that shot on purpose. And some-day you will be a better ruler than your father because of it. A leader's pride should never come before the good of his people—something your father has never realized. The crowds only cheer for him because they fear him, not because they love him."

Dinah stayed silent.

"I'll let you rest until the feast tonight," Harris mur-mured, leaning over to give her a kiss on her head. She would have fallen asleep angry had it not been for the memory of Wardley's honeyed smile, the passionate look on his face as he had gazed at her. Instead, his beauty carried her softly into a place of silence, where her hungry fears lay waiting.

Dinah dreamed she was floating through a black ink, weightless, without the confines of her body. Tiny sparks of white light pulsated on the sides of her vision. They circled and danced while she wavered between consciousness and slumber. Dinah was aware of something malevolent slowly swimming through the black mist toward her. It was just out of reach, but it was fearful and hungry. Dinah realized with a start that she was actually hanging upside down, her hair undulating in the bright stars.

The inky sky throbbed and turned into a silver liquid.

Dinah spun in the air, clawing to upright herself. Clocks and various pieces of furniture drifted past, buoyed on an invisible river. The black gave a second shudder, and she was now floating in a mirror. The murderous pursuer was close—she could feel it now. It was almost on top of her. Icy-cold fingernails clutched at her stomach and breasts. Struggling, Dinah righted herself, rising up over her feet until the tip of her nose brushed the soft mirror. It parted like water. There was no one behind her. Her own arms clutched at her body. Her black eyes opened wide as she looked at her own reflection. *She* was the darkness.

Dinah lurched out of bed with a start. She was drenched with sweat, her arms flailing in the cold night air. Emily stood up from the rocking chair near the bed.

"Everything all right, Princess?"

"Yes, yes. Thank you, Emily. What time is it?"

Emily put down her knitting. "We should probably dress for the feast. Anything in mind, Your Highness?"

Dinah stared out the window at the shifting Wonderland stars, her mind lingering on the dream. "Something light. Absolutely no wool."

♥

Dinah usually disliked feasts. After the endless and mind-numbing pageantry that was the seating of the lords and ladies, the highborn Cards, the squires, and the advisers, she and the rest of the royal family were finally seated behind the King's Table, which was no ordinary piece of stone. The ends of the thick obsidian table curled at the tips, its razor-sharp points the source of more than a few bloodied limbs. The King of Hearts was seated on a raised platform near the middle of the table, his crown resting beside his enormous goblet. His blond mustache was already stained with cherry wine, giving him the look of a crazed cannibal. Dinah sat at his left, Vittiore on his right, looking luminous as always in a form-fitting gown the color of ripe blueberries. Her bright-blue eyes radiated out from her petite face, striking dead the heart of every man in Wonderland. Nary a Card could walk by her without being entranced by her ethereal presence.

The king sat back in his chair and gave a loud burp. "More wine!" he demanded.

Cheshire leaned over her father, hovering as always. He was whispering in her father's ear, aiding as the king's eyes darted around the room, taking in friends, foes, and fools. The squires poured more wine into his massive goblet, and he downed it greedily with one hand, the other hand always resting on his Heartsword. Her father saw enemies in many places, in every house, in every distant and seemingly absurd lineage leading to the throne. Yurkei assassins were everywhere, he believed, each one trying to steal his crown. Emily had spilled to Dinah that rumors abounded about her father's paranoia. That he slept with his Heartsword. That six guards stood watch while he slept. That he truly trusted only Cheshire.

Dinah pushed the oily emu breast around her plate, covering it with seeds and sprouts. She wasn't hungry in the least, and by her count she would have to sit here for another four hours, a frozen smile plastered across her face. Vittiore gave a tinkling laugh at something her father said, and Dinah leaned over to give her a reprimanding look. Cheshire rewarded Vittiore with a pointed smile from above her father's head. Dinah fought the urge to fling her plate at him as bile filled her throat. She could remember being very young—before her mother died—and seeing Cheshire for the first time. With black hair and eyebrows, Cheshire had been young but just as devious looking. His hand had rested on the king's shoulder, had squeezed hard as Dinah approached them both, toddling on little legs. She looked up into the king's face with happy anticipation and saw nothing but simmering anger. He scared her. Wasn't this her father? The man who loved her mother? His blue eyes ran over her, searching for something he did not find. His mouth contorted first with confusion and then disgust. He pushed her back roughly.

"Remove her from my sight. Don't bring her around anymore," he said to Harris, and two Cards gently pulled her away from him. Dinah gave a scream and kicked the first one in the shin. The second Heart Card grabbed for her, and she twisted away from him too.

Crying, she screamed for her father into empty air as Harris wrapped his arms around her waist to restrain her. "Father! Father!"

The King of Hearts walked past her without a second look, his black cloak brushing over her face as he passed her, beyond her. Cheshire followed behind him, his head bowed. Dinah was short enough to see the satisfied smile stretched across his long face. Even as a young child, she suspected that somehow this clever sliver of a man had turned her father's mind against her. His child, the one he was supposed to love but never did. She smiled up at Cheshire, while vowing in her heart that the first thing she would do as queen after her father had passed away or she had married would be to send Cheshire to the Black Towers forever. Of course, he had helped her the day Vittiore arrived by showing her the tunnels, but that was for his own purposes. With Cheshire, one could be sure of it. He was not a man to underestimate.

The hours ticked by slowly as the crowd became more intoxicated with drink and the lights slowly dimmed. Gay laughter and the delicious scent of tarts wrapped like lovers around those who sat and enjoyed the feast. Dinah was bored. She glanced over at her father, who was roaring with laughter along with Xavier Juflee. The King of Hearts did not notice Dinah staring, nor did he notice Vittiore gazing sadly off into the distance, looking at something Dinah could not see. She followed Vittiore's gaze to the back of the room, but there was only the trace of a shadow, no one. Vittiore cast her eyes down, blushing. There was some movement in the periphery of her vision, and Dinah jerked out of her trance and looked down at the table.

Her plate was gone, and in its place was a steaming slice of berry loaf on a delicately thin plate. She blinked in shock. She had not seen the extra plate put down in front of her, and that was alarming in itself. Scrawled in lovely looping letters, someone had written "Eat Me" in raspberry jam on the side of the plate. Bewildered, she looked around, but there was no one acting suspicious, no one looking mischievous in the corner. There were only hundreds of people eating, dancing, and boasting with excitement about their own croquet games of that afternoon. Wardley was making his way to the other side of the room, drinking heavily out of a gigantic silver stein; Harris was talking with the Master of Music; and Charles would never be let anywhere near the royal feast.

She returned her eyes to the message on her plate: "Eat Me." Was this an insult? A threat? Poison? Dinah quickly smeared the words with her silver spoon. Her every breath bursting with curiosity, she raised her fork and brought it down into the loaf. She heard the clink of metal on glass, and found a minuscule glass vial, smaller than a spool of thread. Hands trembling, she picked up the vial, keeping her hands low over her plate. The cork came out easily and a tiny piece of paper slid into her waiting fingertips. She looked around again.

The party continued to escalate. Fat white birds were running up and down the tables, being fed by amused guests. As always, no one cared about the king's strange, black-haired daughter. Her hands shook as she unrolled the paper, wondering who could have possibly sent it. Five words, written in a lilting script, graced the square of parchment: *Faina Baker, the Black Towers.* Scribbled next to the words was a tiny picture of a triangle with a wave underneath it. The symbol was vaguely familiar, although Dinah couldn't quite put her finger on it and didn't have time to think about it at this moment. She turned the paper over. Nothing. The thudding of her heart was so loud that she was sure the entire room could hear it, yet no one even looked in her direction. Dinah closed her eyes, committing the name, the symbol, and the words to memory. Then she did as her plate instructed and ate the words, the paper pasty and tasteless on her tongue.

Seven

The stars were scattered that evening—sprinkled north over the Todren and also to the south, where they hung in vertical lines over the Darklands. Dinah stood alone on her balcony, wrapped in a thick sheepskin blanket.

"Your Highness, you'll freeze out there!" nagged Emily from her chambers. Dinah rolled her eyes and silenced her servant with an upraised hand.

"Emily, I'm fine! I am warm enough; the winter is almost over."

Emily made a face and silently retreated. Dinah turned

her head back to the sky.

"Faina Baker, the Black Towers." She murmured the words to herself, again and again. She couldn't imagine what those words meant, only that she felt—*no, she knew*—that they were something of great meaning and consequence. She had been waiting for that tiny scroll all her life, without knowing it. The unspoken thread of unease that followed her every step in this palace—it had origins. It was present at the croquet game, at the feast, in the whispers of Cards and the court, especially since Vittiore had arrived. Was this tiny paper perhaps her answer, something to put her one step ahead?

Who was Faina Baker? What did she know? And most important, why was she in the Black Towers? Dinah bit at her lip, a nervous habit. Contrary to what she had told Emily, there was quite a bitter chill in the late-winter air; it ripped through her blankets as though they were as thin as linen. She gave a shiver. It was time. Dinah pulled a long burgundy scarf, embroidered with tiny pink flowers, out from beneath her blanket. She reached over the edge of the balcony and looped it around a tiny iron rung on the bottom of the railing. The scarf unfurled itself in the whipping wind, a red ribbon against the black sky.

She went inside, took her tea and bath in silence, and watched the steam gather in her dressing room. Harris and Emily retired for the night to their separate sleeping quarters, and Dinah paced back and forth in front of her windows. Patience had never been her virtue, and when she could wait no longer, she walked out to the balcony and stuck her head over the edge. She squinted until she saw it: Wardley's scalloped silver shield, bearing a kneeling Corning, propped up against a water trough outside the armory.

Dinah's skin gave a happy ripple—Wardley was coming! They had communicated in this manner since she was a little girl. Wardley was always outside by the stables, while Dinah was confined by lessons in the Royal Apartments, so they arranged the simplest form of the message: a shield or a scarf meant, "I need to see you." The other would then put up a reply, and the message was complete. Dinah pulled a simple plum nightgown over her thin tunic and fastened her cloak over it. Pressing her ear to the door, she listened for the Heart Cards to make their way down to the end of the wing.

Their metal footsteps grew fainter until they disappeared completely. Dinah knew it was a matter of minutes before they came back around. Stepping quietly, she slipped out the door and ran down the hall, the marble freezing cold on her bare feet. She made her way down the stone servant steps at the end of the wing, and from there began winding her way through different hallways toward the Heart Chapel.

When his reign first began, her father had ordered the construction of a tiny alcove that overlooked the Heart Chapel. While most found it bewildering that he would make any changes to this ancient room, one that beamed with light and whimsical architecture, the King of Hearts pressed on, though the construction included the destruction of a magnificent old lute that had been sealed into the outer wall. The alcove was nicknamed "the Box." Its purpose was to enlighten and change the hearts of peasants by blessing them with the gift of worshipping inside the chapel, while still keeping them away from members of the court and the royal family. The king believed that granting peasants, undesirables, and orphans audience with royalty would someday inspire great things in a person of low standing.

Every Sunday, peasants were rounded up by the Cards and brought to the Box. They were forced to participate in the service at the Heart Chapel, and then given bread and soup, and sent on their way. After their departure, the Box would receive a thorough cleaning, so that it might be cleared for the next group of woodworkers, butchers, ladies of the night, or fishmongers. Dinah thought it the most terribly condescending idea—did the townspeople really desire to be yanked from their work to worship with those who were gifted with so much? Still, she was grateful that her father had unknowingly provided a private place for Wardley to meet her inside the castle.

As a princess, Dinah was never alone for very long, and she was rarely able to go anywhere in the palace anymore without dozens of people noticing. Just in the last few weeks, Heart Cards had begun accompanying her in places she usually occupied alone: the library, the kitchens, the atrium. Harris said it was because her coronation was drawing near and thus her father had ordered extra protection around her. To Dinah, it was a nuisance she had to learn to tolerate.

Her breath catching in her throat, Dinah pulled open

the huge doors to the Heart Chapel. She was lucky tonight—normally there was a watch, but he must have been away on rounds. She slipped inside. There was something eerie about the vast, shadowy space, empty as a tomb and just as cold. Mosaic walls glittered in the darkness, and she could make out the forms of shrouded stone figures fighting, embracing, and ruling: the Wonderland gods. The chapel's grandeur made her feel small and exposed. Her footsteps seemed to bounce across the floor like cannon blasts as the sounds ricocheted off the columns and walls. Dinah stopped to catch her breath and found herself staring up at the red heart-shaped window that graced the back of the chapel. Fine gold cranes were strung end to end before the heart so that it swallowed them whole, their wings only a spot on its mass.

Dinah stood alone in the darkness, feeling like the cranes—swallowed whole by this room, by the throne, by her father and the palace. She longed to rule—to take the seat next to her father, and she, the Queen of Hearts, would rule over Wonderland with strength and courage—but she feared what it would take to get there. When she married, her father would not easily give up his throne to her husband.

Her black eyes narrowed as she stared up at the brilliant red window, which cast red light on her face. The altar seemed to pulse with crimson. *When I am queen*, she told herself, *all my doubts will disappear, and my father will embrace me again. He will see that I was born to be a queen, and I will be a better queen than he was a king.*

Dinah heard the soft padding of footsteps, and something changed in the air. A soft ripple moved the banners and tapestries that draped the wall, and Dinah was suddenly filled with the dreadful sense that someone was watching her. She turned, but there was only darkness around her—an empty, holy space, and only the eyes of the gods were upon her. She gave a sniff. The air smelled strange—a heady mix of earth and brawn. Behind her, a door clicked and she heard sauntering footsteps echoing through the chapel. *Wardley*. She sighed with relief and reluctantly turned her back to the altar and walked the long length of the aisle until she was parallel to the door. With only the moonlight that filtered in from the red heart window, her strong hands found the wooden ladder that led up to the Box. Dinah gave a soft groan and lifted herself up onto the bottom rung. Wardley poked his face out from the top of the ladder.

"Hurry up! You are slower than a moss-eating bug."

Dinah shot him an angry look and continued to carefully climb, splinters driving into her bare feet. Once she reached the top, she was greeted with the hint of a foul stench: waste, oil, and rotting vegetables—the smell of poverty. Whoever was supposed to clean the Box after the last event didn't. Standing, she brushed her fingers through her tangled hair and straightened her cloak. Wardley stood in front of her, dressed in his practice clothes—a loose, white-linen shirt, dark red pants, and black riding boots. His shirt was opened across the chest, and Dinah could see the gleam of his sweaty skin in the moonlight. Her heart knocked trickily in her chest, and she forced herself to look away.

Wardley gave her a quick hug. "Ugh, you smell awful."

Dinah punched his arm. "It's the Box. Stop it."

"That felt like a swift breeze blowing over my skin," he chided, smiling. Dinah felt the earth tremble. "Try again."

He held out his arm. Dinah struck him with all her might. He winced. "All right, that did actually hurt. Keep working on your sword arm. Someday your father will train you to use the Heartsword."

"Not likely, but it's a nice sentiment."

They sat together on a tattered wooden bench that reeked of fish.

"So, what did you need to tell me?" Wardley asked. "You should have just come to the stables in a few days. It's a lot easier than sneaking around here. Have you noticed that there are Heart Cards everywhere now? It's getting ridiculous, all the men that bear the uniform. Your father doesn't care anymore if they are qualified or good men; he just wants bodies in cloaks." Wardley made a disgusted sound. The constant lowering of requirements to become a Heart Card was something that he lamented often.

"At least they're not Spades."

He looked over at her and saw the seriousness in her eyes. His smile faded. "Dinah, what is it?"

Dinah brought her face close to Wardley's ear. Just being this near to him made it hard to breathe, but they had much to talk about. To any observer, they would look like young lovers, whispering words of endearment. "Yesterday someone gave me a note. It was at the feast, and it was slipped into my berry loaf. It said 'Eat Me.'"

Wardley pulled back from her, his face riddled with concern. He took her face in his hands and tilted it so he could look clearly at her. "You didn't eat it, did you? Dinah, that could have been poison."

Dinah shook her head. "No, no, of course not. I didn't eat it. But I did break it open. And this was inside." She reluctantly pulled back from him and removed the tiny vial from her cloak pocket. "There used to be a piece of paper inside of it. I read it, and then I ate that."

Wardley's eyes widened.

She continued. "On the note it said, 'Faina Baker, the Black Towers.' And then it had a triangle symbol."

Wardley looked at the ceiling, considering. "Faina Baker, I've never heard that name before. Have you?"

Dinah shook her head. "Never. I've been thinking about it all afternoon, but no. I've never heard of her either."

Wardley took the tiny vial out of her fingers and peered at it in the moonlight. "What do you think it means?"

Dinah wrung her hands together. "I truly don't know, but I can't shake the feeling that it's something important."

"You can't know that, Dinah. This could be a trap. Someone plotting against the king, someone plotting against you. Your father has many enemies. It could be a Yurkei assassin."

"I know that. I do." She pulled herself closer to him, her skin pressing against his, her mouth against his ear. "I can't explain it, but I need to find her. Faina. This note wasn't sent in malice, I can *feel* that."

Wardley took her hand in his, and a million stars shot over her skin. "Dinah, I know you want to believe this. I just don't know if it is wise. Your coronation grows closer every day, and maybe this is just you being nervous to take the throne."

Dinah lifted her black eyes and stared at his face. "Do you trust me?"

"Of course. You are my best friend," he assured her, giving a nervous laugh, caught off guard by her intensity.

"Then help me do this. Wardley, something is amiss. I can feel it. There is a lurking, a presence, a danger, something *bad* is happening. And someone is trying to help us. I *need* to speak with Faina Baker, and I need your help to do it."

Wardley shook his head. "Getting into the Black Towers will be impossible. You're the princess; they track your every move. And even if they didn't, you can't just break into the Black Towers. They're swarming with Clubs." He lowered his voice. "And gods know what wickedness we will find in there. You've heard the stories. Some things can never be erased from one's mind. The Black Towers are a place of violence. Torture. Sickness. The depravity of the kingdom is held there, and you're willing to risk going in, just for a name. A name that might mean nothing; nothing more than a traitor waiting in the dark with a dagger behind his back. Do you truly believe this woman has all the answers? What answers are you seeking? And if she does, why is she in the Black Towers?"

He gave a sigh. "Dinah, listen to me. Criminals go to the Black Towers. Criminals and liars and murderers and people who your father needs to disappear. It is not a place for a princess." He kissed her knuckle chastely. "My dear friend and future queen, please abandon this."

Dinah's head was swirling. She hadn't considered all the things that Wardley had said, but it didn't matter. She knew the slithering feeling making its way up her spine, day by day. "As the Princess of Wonderland, I order you to help me."

Wardley gave her an exasperated look. "You wouldn't do that. Besides, I don't have to listen to you. You're not the queen yet."

"But I will be."

"And on that day, I will listen to you."

Through the filtered moonlight, Dinah looked at him—her friend, her playmate. Someday maybe her lover. "I cannot do this without you, Wardley. We've always dreamed and imagined what the Black Towers would look like; well, here's our chance."

Wardley abruptly stood, grabbing her roughly by the shoulder. "This isn't a game, Dinah. This isn't us playing 'Black Towers' in the rose garden, ducking behind the bushes. There could be serious consequences. Do you want to lose your crown? Do you want me to lose my head?"

Dinah dropped her head with a whisper. "I know I am asking too much of you. But this is something I must do, with or without you. There is something else. The symbol on the note—the triangle made of waves? I've seen it before."

With a finger, Dinah drew the symbol in the dirt-lined floor. Wardley looked at it blankly. "What is that?"

"It took me all night to remember, but I know where I've seen this symbol before. It's etched in the tunnels below the palace. I remember, there were three hidden tunnels. One led to the Great Hall, one led to just outside the gates on the east side, and there was another one marked with this emblem." She pointed to it. "Before, I thought it was a picture of a mountain—the Yurkei Mountains—a sign marking that the tunnel went in that direction. But I was wrong. It's the symbol for the Black Towers. I think that tunnel leads into the Black Towers."

Wardley scratched his chin, stubble already starting to grow back from that morning's shave. "But how can we be sure?"

"We can't."

"And we wouldn't know which tower Faina Baker was in to begin with."

"That's correct."

Wardley now paced angrily, his boots stirring up a small

dust cloud. Dinah could see that he was actively fighting his own curiosity. "How would we even get into the Great Hall? It's guarded round the clock. Just for my amusement, let's say we get in there, and then we use the tunnels to get in. Then what? We can't just stroll around the Black Towers, the princess and I, out for a tour."

"We can take care of that," breathed Dinah. "I have a plan."

"Let's just say that we get in. We find Faina Baker in one of *seven* towers. We talk to her, have some tea, she tells us all sorts of secrets. Then what? We just stroll out onto the Iron Web? Make our way back to the tunnels?"

Dinah gave a shrug. "We have a lot to plan; I'm not saying it will be easy."

"Easy? It's madness. This is a suicide mission. And for what?"

Dinah raised herself up from the bench and took his arm gently. "For the future queen to have the upper hand before her coronation. For not wondering what if? For answers that have never been given to me, and never will be. For the possibility of understanding *something* about this place."

"And if I lose my head?" Wardley asked.

"Then I will be very sorry," she said. "It is a lovely head."

She placed her hand on his cheek. She felt so near to him—his physical presence was overwhelming. She took in his hot breath washing over her face, the sweat shimmering on his brow, his curly chocolate hair pushed haphazardly back from his forehead. Without thinking, she pressed her lips against his. They were cool and soft, and hers felt warm and hungry against them. White lights exploded underneath Dinah's eyelids and she opened her mouth slightly under his. His lips remained still as he jerked back in surprise, his hands on her shoulders.

"Dinah, I—" He didn't have time to finish. Something moved in the darkness below. They heard the shuffling of feet, an unexplained whoosh of air. The ladder gave a wooden creak. In one rapid movement, Wardley drew his sword and pushed Dinah protectively behind him. His blade gleamed in the moonlight. "Someone's here," he whispered. "Don't move. Stay behind me."

Fear froze them both as a chill crept upon Dinah's skin, a breath caught in her throat. Neither of them moved for several minutes, barely daring to breathe. From the darkness, the sounds of long, easy breaths drifted up the ladder. And then, just when the sound of her roaring heart was so loud she was sure it was drowning out the entire palace, the presence disappeared. The malignant air was sucked out of the room, although the feeling of being watched lingered. Dinah wondered if whoever it was had been there the entire time. Wardley replaced his sword.

"They're gone. They couldn't have heard us, could they?"

Dinah shook her head. Suddenly, there was a bang, and they both jumped toward each other as the doors of the Heart Chapel burst open and three Cards marched in for their nightly rounds. Dinah and Wardley ducked down into the Box to avoid being seen. She felt a rush of relief at the Cards' presence, even though she lay on the stinking floor to avoid their gaze. Wardley looked over at her with wide eyes.

"There was someone there," he whispered. "I heard him."

Dinah gave a nod. Wardley gave her a look of defeat, his face coated with a fine layer of brown dust. "Fine," he snapped. "I'll go to the Black Towers with you, but I'm not going to enjoy it. You're right—something is amiss. I hear whispers at the stables, and among the Cards. A Spade told me that the king fears for his life and is gathering his Cards all around him. But why?"

"You'll go with me then?"

Wardley nodded, his ear cocked, listening to the watch. Dinah was glad to see them go, but the mortification of kissing him slowly returned now that the danger had gone.

"Wardley, I'm sorry about the—"

He cut her off. "Don't worry about it."

They heard the doors to the chapel slam shut, and suddenly they were alone again. Wardley grabbed her hand and yanked Dinah to her feet. "It's time to go. Now." They climbed quickly down the ladder, Wardley wrapping his arms around Dinah's waist at the bottom and putting her on the ground. "Go, now. Go back to your chambers. Take the servants' passage. We will talk about this later. Come see me at the stables tomorrow. We are not going to meet here again. Ever. I can't believe I'm going to do this."

Dinah didn't need to be told twice, but she didn't want

to leave him, not while he was so upset. "Wardley, you don't have to go to the Black Towers. I see now that I shouldn't have asked you. But I must go. I am not a child anymore, and I need to know what is happening in my kingdom. Can you understand?"

Wardley glanced over at her like she was insane. "If you are going to be the Queen of Hearts," he deadpanned, "you should try not to be so daft. I have no choice. If you go, I will go. You're not as good with a sword as you think. Besides, if you die, your father will have my head one way or another. It might as well be for doing something brave."

Dinah gave him a quick smile. "Brave? Or a fool's errand?"

Dinah had played Wardley—she knew he could never resist an adventure. Wardley glanced around the empty room. It was silent.

"We'll make a plan later, but we will take our time doing it. Now, *go*."

She wanted to kiss him again, kiss him always, forever. But that was not happening tonight, so she picked up her skirt and ran as fast as she could to her bedchamber. It wasn't until she lay in her bed that evening, replaying the kiss in all its awkward loveliness, the cool Wonderland breeze dancing over her skin, that she realized they had left the vial in the Box, along with a drawing in the dust of a wavy triangle. It was there alone, in the darkness, waiting to be discovered.

Eight

Exactly one month since her whispered conversation in the Box, Dinah rubbed the sleep out of her eyes as she glanced wearily at the ticking clock tucked into her bookcase. *Today is the day*, she thought, pushing herself onto her elbows. She sat up in bed, holding her cool palms against her warm cheeks, and allowed herself several deep breaths. *I must be calm or this will never work*, she thought. *It must appear as every other day to everyone except Wardley and me.* She gave an exaggerated yawn as Emily came bustling in with her fluffy bathing towels.

"How are you, Your Highness?"

"Just fine, thank you."

The morning dragged on: an elaborate bath followed by dressing and chatting idly with Harris and Emily. As Emily laced up the back of her gown, Dinah cleared her throat. "I've been invited to have tea today with Vittiore. I think I might attend in the afternoon."

Emily stopped lacing. "With Vittiore? But . . . ?" Emily was well aware of Dinah's deep hatred of Vittiore.

"It might not be a terrible idea to get to know her better. I'm to be queen soon, and I should make peace with her. I can't resent her forever. She is my subject."

Dinah felt her voice edge up as the lie felt sour against her tongue. Harris stared at her from across the room in shock.

"I'll make sure to dismiss Palma and Nanda." Emily bit her lip angrily. She hated Vittiore's two silly, stupid serving girls, which made Dinah love Emily even more. The servants never spoke to each other, not even on the palace rounds of gathering sheets, dresses, and daily linens. Dinah didn't understand the deep hatred that the women had for each other, but for today at least, it was perfect that they wouldn't even look one another in the eye. Harris hopped in happily from the other side of the room.

"Did I hear that you will be taking tea with Vittiore today? Dinah, that is a magnificent idea. How wonderful! It is time that you two put aside your differences. You might see that she is the sister you always wanted."

Ribbons tightened around Dinah's ribs as Emily laced her up.

"A little lighter, Emily. I don't want to seem strained at tea today."

Emily gave a frown. "I didn't think about that, Your Highness. My apologies." There was a heartbeat of silence, and then the pressure was relieved. "Why don't we skip the corset for today, especially if you will be seated for a long period of time. But let's go with a brilliant gown then, something that will remind the duchess that you are the future queen." Emily opened Dinah's white wardrobe and pulled out a magenta silk gown, all rosettes and layers. "This will make your black hair look radiant."

Dinah made a face—to do otherwise would be out of character.

"Don't frown, Princess, just put it on."

As the gown slipped over her head, Dinah cleared her throat. "I'll be at the library all morning doing private studies with Monsignor Wol-vore."

Wol-vore was the language tutor. Dinah spent several days a week with him, learning to mimic the tongue of the Yurkei Mountain tribes and to hum the strange lilting sounds of the Western Slope accents. It was utterly useless in Dinah's eyes, and mind-numbingly boring. That particular day, however, Monsignor Wol-vore would be visiting his mistress, a lovely lady of the court who lived just outside the palace. Wardley was finding that gold and gems bought a bounty of information on the various dark vices of the court.

"That sounds lovely, Dinah, just lovely. I am so proud of you."

Harris looked so happy, all puffed up and red-cheeked. A stab of guilt shot through her. Dinah stared at herself in the mirror. *Black eyes, many lies*, she thought. Dinah cleared her throat.

"Both of you—I officially free you of all your duties for the day. Emily, you should go visit your family, and

Harris—what better time to take in the rose garden or play some croquet? I heard our white vendela roses are starting to bloom. . . ."

Harris's eyes lit up. "I suppose I should. A bit of nature acts as a tonic for the soul."

That was easy, she thought. Emily finished dressing Dinah, and she quickly ate her breakfast, making sure to have double helpings of both eggs and sweet peach breads. She would need it. As she headed out the door, Dinah grabbed a thin muslin bag.

"My books," she mumbled.

Emily and Harris didn't even look up. Dinah could see that they were excited at the prospect of a day with no responsibilities, which was rare for servants and guardians. *Two down*, Dinah thought, as she made a point of taking her time walking to the Great Hall, greeting Cards as they passed, and any court members who always seemed to be lollygagging in the hallway without purpose. She would be seen today, wearing this ridiculous gown and seeming oddly friendly. Dinah strolled past the Great Hall and noted the three Heart Cards standing watch in front of the door.

Fellen, Roxs, and Thatcher, just as she and Wardley had cal-
culated. Dinah gave them a gentle nod as she passed.

Guarding the Great Hall was a low honor among Heart
Cards. Those with the most skill and loyalty guarded the
king, then Cheshire, then Dinah, and so on down the court
line. Those who were either new to the Cards or had a questionable record of service guarded the palace's many doors
and rooms. Nothing happened in the Great Hall most days of
the Wonderland year, and so the Heart Cards sent to guard
its doors and hallways were ruthlessly mocked. As Dinah
walked past them, they bowed lazily. Dinah removed a small
pouch from her bag. Then she stumbled, sending the little
bag flying out in front of her. A wealth of gold coins—more
than enough to feed their families for a year—spilled out in
front of them. The muslin satchel stayed tight on her shoulders. She saw Roxs's eyes light up. Of course they would: he
had not one, but two families to feed. He bent down to help
her pick up the coins, and Dinah saw him slyly pocket a few.
Perfect, she thought.

"I'm so sorry. So clumsy."

"'Tis never a problem, my lady."

Dinah swiftly picked up the remaining coins, making sure to give the men a clean glimpse of all the coins inside the bag. *The price of a necklace*, she thought guiltily, *just one of the many jewels that sit idly in my drawer, more than enough to feed a family.* She often found herself feeling shame at such things. She nodded her head at Roxs, and then at the other Cards.

"Thank you. Good day." Lowering her eyes, she made herself fidgety and breathless before them. She hesitated a second and leaned forward, letting her hair swing down over her face, her voice dropping to an urgent whisper. "Could you please tell me where the cloak room is?" Dinah absolutely knew where the cloak room was.

Roxs gave a nod. "Not sure why you would need that, Your Highness. You aren't even wearing a cloak."

Dinah put a hand on her hip. "It's none of your business, and above your station to ask."

Roxs's eyes narrowed. No Heart Card liked being reprimanded by the royal family—it was an ultimate shame from those they swore to protect. "Forgive me, my lady. I will walk you there."

"No. Just tell me how to get there. I can walk there myself. Time is of the essence."

Dinah could see the confusion playing across their faces. *Why is she in a hurry to get to the cloak room?*

"Follow this hall, past the oratory, and around the corner. It's a small door on the right, across from the servants' privy. There is an iron-and-glass window on the front of the door."

Dinah clutched her purse tightly against her chest and let a blush rise to her cheeks. "Thank you." She hurried quickly past the Cards. The cloak room was very simple to find. Dinah had been there many times as a child, retrieving a winter cloak for her or for Charles. It was a long room, filled from ceiling to floor with every kind of cloak in every kind of color, all for the royal family or their distinguished guests. Steam hissed out from a fountain in the middle of the room—a porcelain whale that spewed mist periodically, making sure that the cloaks were always warm and soft, whatever the weather. Dinah quickly found a simple, brown, hooded cloak.

She set her muslin bag down on the ground, yanking

open its cords. Inside was a gray cotton dress, a tiny white heart embroidered on the sleeve. It was the kind of dress a maid or servant might wear on her day off. Dinah had swiped it from Emily earlier that month. She quickly shrugged out of her elaborate magenta gown, the ruffles swimming around her like puffy clouds. She carefully folded it and placed it into the bag. The cloak room door opened, and she gave a shriek as she stood with only a thin white slip on.

"It's just me," Wardley hissed.

Dinah turned her back to him and started to pull the gray dress over her head. Wardley crossed the room. "No. Wait. Leave it off."

Her heart felt like it was plunged into icy water.

"They will be in here any minute. I saw their faces when I asked for the cloak room." He shook his head and began grumbling. "The king should never have men like this in his service. In his attempt to build a strong set of Cards, he has taken even the worst of men. His ever-lowering standards are weakening the kingdom."

"Shhh—" Dinah heard heavy footsteps and the clanking of metal outside the door. Quickly, Wardley wrapped his hand around her waist and pulled her against him. His lips traced down her neck, his breath scorching as it passed over her creamy skin. She closed her eyes and surrendered, aware of how every curve of her body showed through the thin fabric, so close to him, so close to being just her skin pressed against his. The heat from his body washed over her, their breath becoming one in the small space between them. Dinah's body pulled toward him as she raised her lips to meet his.

Wardley watched her silently as he gathered her thick black hair in his hands, his eyes tracing down her bodice before he looked away sharply. "Let's not oversell it," he murmured.

The door burst open. The three Cards stood in front of them, grinning like fools. Roxs stepped forward. "Well, well, Princess; it seems you have acquired a taste for the stable boy."

"Get out," growled Wardley. "Don't come near the princess."

"You should have taken that advice yourself. Seems like you have quite the handful there. She's not to my taste—that leans more to the Lady Vittiore and those blond curls—but there is a certain appeal to her. I heard she's feisty like her father and crazy like her brother. She has fire in the blood."

Roxs circled Dinah, his lecherous eyes taking in entirely too much of her. "So, you're plucking the princess. This secret tryst of yours, what's it worth to you?"

Dinah gulped. "What do you mean?"

"I mean, how much gold was in that purse of yours? Two hundred? Three hundred? That would buy me land, girl, and food for my families."

Wardley laid his hand across his sword. "You may not blackmail the princess. The king will have your head on Execution Day for this."

"Well, let's go tell him, shall we?" Roxs headed to the door, his two henchmen grinning like idiots beside him.

"Wait," Dinah said quietly. "How much do you want?"

"Everything that's in that purse, miss, and nothing less to buy our silence."

"That is a fortune," breathed Dinah angrily.

"And that's what I'm asking."

Dinah reached for her bag.

Wardley stepped forward. "Let the lady and me discuss this, then we'll talk."

"Some lady," grunted Fellen, but the Cards stepped out, shutting the door behind them. She could hear their greedy laughter outside the door.

"That went well," whispered Wardley. He pulled Dinah close to him again and pressed his lips against hers.

The Cards barged back in, unable to wait. "Can't keep your hands off each other, eh? I remember being young and lusty—you can't keep your manhood down!"

The Cards jostled with glee. Wardley raised his hand and they fell silent. Even when they assumed he was just a stable boy, he commanded attention. "Here is what we propose. The princess and I never have time to, let's just say, be by ourselves. We will give you all the gold in this purse, along with—"

Dinah pulled out a large amethyst ring. The Cards' eyes lit up.

"This, if you allow us to stay in this room for as long as we desire and make sure that no one, *no one* comes in. That includes you. If anyone asks where the princess is today, you are to say that she is having tea with the Lady Vittiore and studying in the library. You never saw us here. Do you understand? We'll give you the coins now, but the ring we will give you after we are . . . finished." Wardley let a naughty smile play across his face. "And we'll need all day."

Roxs stepped forward. "And why should we do this for you?"

"Because who will the king believe—a drunken Card accused of stealing the princess's gold or his daughter?"

Roxs considered it for a moment. "Done."

Wardley handed him the bag. "Remember. No one comes in or out. We want at least until nightfall together. When we come out, you will get the ring."

Fellen gave a snort. "You think you can last that long, son?"

Wardley leveled him with a gaze. "Without a doubt."

The Three Cards exchanged an envious look and backed out of the room. "We must keep our watch over the Great Hall, but we'll hear you if you sneak out. Don't cheat us, boy!"

"Fine," replied Dinah. "Keep your promise and I will

keep mine, and I will not take your heads for your silence."

The Cards left. Wardley glanced at Dinah with a bemused grin. "Men of questionable character can always be trusted in situations that involve gold."

Dinah didn't have time for banter. "Did you bring the breastplate? The uniform?"

"I did."

Wardley also had a bag. Out of it he pulled a white breastplate with the gray Club symbol etched on it. He slipped the armor over a gray tunic and fastened his black cloak with a tiny glittering Club pin at his right shoulder. "How do I look?" he whispered.

"Like a Club," Dinah replied. "Me?"

"Like a servant, only cleaner."

Dinah quickly braided her hair and then started pushing back the cloaks in the corner of the room. They moved cloak after cloak aside until they saw it: a small wooden door, expertly camouflaged with the wood around it.

"I still can't believe this is in here," Dinah whispered, running her hand over the minute cracks.

Wardley nodded. "This was how your great-grandfather

snuck out of the Great Hall to meet his Yurkei mistress, a serving girl of the king. The tunnels through the castle are well-known among the Heart Cards."

"Except mine," Dinah said softly.

"Except yours." Wardley took a deep breath and pushed open the door. "Let out a cry."

"What?"

"Let out a cry, a loud one."

Dinah did as she was told.

"That should keep them satisfied for a while." Wardley laughed. "Let's go." They ducked under the door.

The passage—a sort of hallway between wooden wall brackets—led them directly into a niche in the stone that pushed out into the Great Hall. Checking that the massive room was empty, they quickly ran up the steps and past the throne. Dinah led Wardley into the narrow foyer bordering her father's privy.

"This is the way into the tunnels? Through the privy?"

Dinah didn't reply. She was too busy turning over tapestries. The last one, an elaborate work of art depicting her father's victory over Mundoo—the chief of the

Yurkei—showered them with dirt and dead spiders as she yanked it back. There, there was the door—the one she remembered from that terrible day when Vittiore had arrived and her father had led her bastard sister out proudly like his prized steed. The day Cheshire had shown her the tunnel and she accidentally wove her way beyond the palace gates.

The door inched open with a loud creak. They slipped through it, making sure to leave the door unlocked behind them. Dinah led Wardley down into the damp stone tunnels that ran parallel to the Great Hall and then, with a sudden plunge, down underneath it. The tunnels were dank and cold, much more unpleasant than the last time Dinah had been down there. The buildup of winter snow around Wonderland had turned them into long, wet slabs of frozen mud and cracked rock. Dinah watched her breath freeze and fall to the ground in front of them with a loud tinkle.

Wardley grabbed a torch from the wall and lit it with his flint. Pink flame danced over his face. "We ought to hurry. You could fall asleep down here and never wake up. The cold is just cold enough . . ." He trailed off, his lips turning a deep shade of blue.

They ran. The tunnel became deeper and colder the farther they spiraled into the frosty earth. Several times Dinah had to backtrack, trying to remember all the twists and turns she had taken six months ago. It was nearly impossible; she had been so deeply wounded that day, running blindly through the weaving catacombs. Did she turn here, at that strange cat etching on the wall? Or was it up there, when the tunnel split into four hallways and then returned to itself? She gave a shiver through her cloak.

"We should have grabbed more layers," Wardley whispered. They had been down in the tunnels for almost an hour by Dinah's pocket watch, lifted easily off Harris the day before. "Are we almost there? Maybe we should head back."

It seemed darker than before, and a sudden rush of panic enveloped Dinah. "I'm not sure. It's so dark down here."

"And cold," added Wardley. "Don't forget cold."

Dinah bit her lip as she took in her surroundings. "It's so much darker because we are deeper underground—the same reason it's getting colder. Hold the torch up to the ceiling."

She looked up and trailed her fingers across the dirt.

Wardley held the torch above her. The light flickered and jumped against shiny black roots running the length of the tunnel. Every once in a while they gave a tiny pulse, as if alive, and they seemed to move ever closer.

Dinah grinned in the darkness. "Roots! That happened the first time. I remember thinking they looked like black bones. We're almost there!"

"I pray you are right," muttered Wardley, his teeth chattering. "Otherwise, we are turning back and I will spend the rest of my day warming my toes by a fire while you feed me tarts."

The stone walls started to narrow; Dinah and Wardley turned sideways as they squeezed through, their faces damp with sweat. They turned one corner and then another, a maze of barely visible walls and dirt. There was a downward slope, and then suddenly they were there. The dirt circle. The collision of the three passageways.

Wardley let out a long breath and waved the torch at the drawings. "Incredible. This is old, Dinah, very old. Ancient."

Dinah ran her fingers over the wavy triangle. "When I was down here before, I thought this was a symbol for the

Yurkei Mountains. But it is so clearly the Black Towers."

Wardley wrapped his hand around her fingers with a friendly squeeze. "You wanted to escape what your father had just done. It makes sense that you wanted it to be the Yurkei Mountains—it was anywhere but where he was."

Dinah's black eyes glittered in the darkness. "Do you have the chains?"

Wardley gave his bag a shake. Dinah heard metal clang against metal. "Let's go, Princess."

"You can't call me that anymore," replied Dinah as she crouched on her hands and knees and began crawling through the tunnel. "Once we get inside, you can call me any name other than that one. Be as cruel as possible." She paused to catch her breath. "Pray that this goes to the Black Towers."

Wardley grunted behind her. "I'm praying that it doesn't."

The tunnel sloped upward steeply, the air growing oddly stifling, almost humid. The warm dirt felt good underneath her freezing palms as they began their ascent.

Nine

Dinah's knees ached when she rose again. Crawling up a steep slope had been much harder than she'd anticipated. Up ahead, light appeared from a narrow hole at the end of the tunnel. Dinah poked her head out and gave a sigh of relief. The smallest flicker of sunlight leaked in from a single rusted window that seemed to be miles above her. They had come to some sort of stone cylinder, and the tunnel went no farther. She looked down. The almost-vertical shaft ended abruptly with a steep drop into a large pool of ice. Wardley pushed up from behind.

"Stop, stop, we could fall!" whispered Dinah frantically. She glanced at her surroundings and found what she was looking for. Jagged stairs led up and away from the drop: mangled teeth that spiraled up the wall of the concave ring.

Wardley wiped his face. "It's warmer in here."

Dinah looked at the ice. "Not warm enough."

"We must be in a hollowed-out grain silo. There are a number of them around the Towers."

Wardley went first, climbing over Dinah and pulling himself up against the wall. "Stay close to the wall. Inch by inch. I see a door up there." He gestured his chin upward. Dinah swallowed. A fall would not kill them, but it would surely break them.

"Don't look down," he instructed Dinah. She did, her eyes following a crooked crack in the ice. Buried up to its waist, frozen forever, was a skeleton. Its bony fingers dug into the ice, the claw marks inches deep. The scream on its face was etched there for eternity, the jawbone hanging grotesquely from its hinge.

Dinah gave a shudder. "Was that . . . ?"

Wardley pressed his body against the wall. "Done

on purpose? Yes. I told you the Black Towers was a brutal place. Club Cards find many ways of extracting information, mostly by torture."

"So that man . . ."

"So that man was probably put down there in the water before the snow arrived and forced to watch as it froze around him. I would guess he's chained to the bottom, at the ankles."

Dinah stared, letting the revulsion wash over her. She shivered. "How is it both humid and cold in here?"

"It's the Black Towers."

Dinah fixed her eyes on the skeleton. Wardley, ever so carefully, reached his fingers under Dinah's chin and turned her head. "Look away."

The thrill of finding their way through the tunnels diminished with each pensive step toward the door, ever mindful of the frozen ground. Dinah heard the cry of enormous Wonderland bats, sometimes known to attack horses. *Don't look up*, she told herself, pressing tighter to the wall. *Don't look up and don't look down, just stay steady.* They climbed silently until they reached a dilapidated wooden door, eaten away by mold and bat droppings.

Wardley turned to Dinah, the flame casting a pink hue on her dark features. "This is it. We can turn back from here, but after we go through this door, we will have to finish what we have started."

Dinah looked at the door with a steely resolve, her stomach churning with fear. Regret was beginning to worm its way into her brain. But then she saw the note, unrolled from its tiny vial, and remembered the feeling that overcame her when she read it—that whatever conspiracy swirling through Wonderland Palace was coming for her eventually, whether she accepted it or not. She looked at Wardley, a brown lock of hair sticking to his sweaty forehead. "Faina Baker, the Black Towers. That's where we are going."

His face fell as he understood that they would not be turning back. "As Your Highness commands. Stay behind me, and whatever you do, for the love of Wonderland gods, do not speak. You can disguise your face and dress, but you speak like a royal and that cannot be undone."

Wardley reached into his bag and clamped iron shackles over her wrists. They were heavier than Dinah had anticipated. "You look a mess," he informed her. Dinah had been purposely careless as she walked and crawled through the tunnels. Her dress was caked with mud. She had soot from the flame smeared across her face and she had let her clean hair run against the tunnel wall. She looked like a commoner—more than a commoner, a criminal.

Dinah gave a shudder in the cold, wet air. "I'm ready."

Wardley drew his eyes to her face, and Dinah saw a fear that matched her own. "We stay together, no matter what happens. You brought your crown?"

Dinah nodded and patted her bag. "Just in case things go wrong." She wrapped her freezing hand around his. The chains gave a slight jangle.

"Here we go," said Wardley. He gave a hard grunt, and the chain mail on his fist broke the aged lock on the door. It fell to the ground with a loud clang. Together they took a deep breath and stepped inside.

The temperature change was immediate and severe. Whereas before they had been freezing, Dinah was soon covered in sweat. The air was thick, humid, and filthy. Pillars of black smoke rose up from below them. They appeared to be in a giant cocoon—a spiraling black tower, wider at the bottom and consistently narrowing toward the top. They were looking out across a wide chasm filled with heavy, dangling chains that twisted down from the cone's point. On either side of them stretched endless cells embedded in the circumference of the tower, one after another, smaller and smaller the higher they went. The smell was inhuman and Dinah gave a loud retch, unable to control herself, followed by another and another. Urine, sweat, human waste, and blood, all mingled together in the thick air.

Wardley bent over her. "Are you going to be all right?"

"I'm your prisoner!" Dinah quietly reminded him in between heaves.

Wardley stood up. "Right. C'mon then." He gave a yank of her chain, and Dinah followed along behind him as they circled their way higher and higher into the tower. High-pitched screams of pain echoed up from below, and Dinah fought the urge to clap her hands over her ears. Wardley yanked her chains so she walked closer beside him.

"I've heard rumors that they torture prisoners on the floor of the tower, but the smallest cells are at the top. The worst criminals are kept in the top cells, so that after their torture sessions, they have to crawl back up the spiral until they can rest." He shook his head. "The crawl is its own form of torture. It's sick."

Dinah's eyes rested with pity upon an old man in a cell they passed, sitting on the floor in his own waste, licking the black, slimy wall. He turned as they walked by. Dinah gave him a sad smile from under her hood. Without warning, the man lunged at her from inside the cell, and managed to grab the edge of her cloak. He pulled her violently against the bars, shaking her back and forth as he reached out to grope her.

"The hearts, the hearts, I love my hearts!"

Dinah felt his rotten breath splash across her face, and she fought another rising wave of nausea. Wardley drew his sword and raised it above the man's gnarled hand. "You will let go of her or you will lose a limb today."

The prisoner laughed in Dinah's face. "Lose a limb, lose a limb, we all will lose our limbs and heads today. . . ."

"Quizzer, let that prisoner go!" boomed a very loud

voice from behind them. The man let go of Dinah with a final shake of his head and sunk back into his celled cave, hissing, "I'll be watching you, my dark-eyed queen, yes I will!"

Dinah stepped back in shock. They turned. A fat man, larger than even her father, waddled up before them. His Club uniform—a thin white tunic overlaid with a gray breastplate and gray wool cape held in place by a club clasp—stretched out to fit his massive girth. Over his breastplate, the Club symbol was encompassed by a much larger skull. She had seen this symbol in a book once or twice; this man was a torturer. Dinah looked at the ground. She felt a slight twitch of fear ripple up Wardley's hand and through her chains.

"Thank you for your aid. I'm to take this filthy wench to the Women's Tower, but we must have taken a wrong turn. I apologize."

The shrill scream of a prisoner circled up from below, followed by pleading whimpers. A tear leaked from Dinah's eye, cutting a clean line through the dirt on her face. Without warning, the torturer reached out and struck her hard across the face. The blow took Dinah's breath away, and she fell to the ground. Wardley looked stunned, unsure what to do.

"Who are you to have sympathy for that man? He is no longer a man. Once you enter the Black Towers, you become a part of them. You belong to the Towers and to the Club Cards. You are the dirt under our feet, the waste in our privy, a slave to the *tree*. Do not weep for that man, for he deserves what he is getting. His screams say that he is thankful for the king's justice, thankful to repay his debt to Wonderland. Soon your screams will say the same thing."

Dinah stared at the ground.

"Where did you say you were taking her, boy?"

"To the Women's Tower. I'm new. I was just transferred here from the Heart Cards."

The man gave a spiteful sniff and spat on the ground. "You look like a Heart Card with that pretty face. Be glad you left. They are a bunch of weak, ignorant bastards who love to boast that they protect the king. Instead, their lives are spent guarding doorways to empty chambers and watching the royal family count their jewels."

On the floor, Dinah wiped the blood from her mouth and thought about the ring hidden in her cloak pocket. Counting indeed.

"Well, at least you have joined a real deck of Cards here." He clapped Wardley on the back. "You're young and strong. You'll do well here, if you learn to stomach the smell and the screams. I'm Yoous, the head torturer of this tower."

A bellow, a sound of pure agony, floated up from below. The Club guard leaned back and closed his eyes. "Ah. I revel in the screams. That sound means that justice has been accepted and that Wonderland is back on its way toward balance and harmony. Learn to love the screams, boy."

Wardley nodded his pale face. Dinah kept her head tilted toward the floor. The prisoner who had so frightened her leered out at her from his cell, licking his lips. "My queen . . ."

"So, where do I take this one, this . . . detriment to society?" Wardley yanked her chains roughly.

The Club gave a loud guffaw. "Did Erinsten send you?"

Wardley raised his lip in a sneer. "Does Erinsten do anything?"

The man gave a laugh and stroked his long mustache. "This is most certainly true. He does not. Well, he should have told you that there is no Women's Tower. All prisoners are housed according to their crime, not their sex. This is the murderers' hive."

The Club began to circle Dinah. "Are you a murderer, my little blackberry tart? Who did you kill? Your lover? Your children?" He pushed her hood back and ran a hand down her thick black braid. "Shiny hair for such a commoner. Were you a whore perhaps? One of the king's whores?"

Wardley pressed a finger against his forehead and rubbed, as if he was remembering something. "Erinsten said that she is to be housed with a Feena Boker, yes, I think that's the name. Or Fina?"

The man stepped back from Dinah with caution. "Faina Baker?"

Wardley snapped his fingers. "Oh yes, that's it, Faina."

"Faina Baker is in here for high treason. She is in the top cell of the Seventh Tower." He peered at Dinah. "That makes you worse than any man in this tower. I'll keep my distance." He leaned forward and trailed his fingers down

Dinah's cheek. "What they do in that tower is worse than death, worse than any torture we do here. I pity you, my pretty."

Wardley gave Dinah a yank, and they started to make their way back down the spiral.

"I wouldn't go that way if I were you. We just gutted a man down there, and you don't want to get blood all over your boots. Take the Iron Web. You better get used to it. Clubs use the web, otherwise we never see the sun."

Yoous picked at his teeth with his huge black fingers. Wardley let out a grunt and began walking back up the spiral, dragging Dinah behind him.

"You're going the wrong way. Oh gods. Here, take this door." He walked between two cells, and a short and narrow hallway opened up before them. It led to a thin metal door.

"No locks?" asked Wardley in disbelief.

Yoous gave a laugh. "You think a prisoner would try to escape the Black Towers? Knowing that there is more torture to come when they get caught? No, no one tries to escape. Besides, they would just escape to the Iron Web, where there are always dozens of Cards going about their day. That or fall to their death. They have no dream of escape. Their minds are worn down by the Towers themselves." He ran his hand across the wall, black and thick and covered with a sticky sap. "Do you know the legend of the Black Towers, son?"

Wardley did, and so did Dinah, but he just shook his head. Yoous took a seat on a decrepit bench, his legs spread wide in Dinah's direction. She looked away.

"They say the towers were here before any of us, before Wonderland proper, even before the Yurkei tribes arrived. They were always here, huge black roots, twisted into a spiral, exactly seven of them. When the Yurkei came upon this land, they worshipped the towers and built their homes around them. Time marched on, and the towers grew thicker and thicker, until they were a massive black tree, stronger than steel, immune to fire and ax. We carve the doors out where there are gaps in the roots. The Yurkei called them 'Meis Yur,' meaning 'the Old Root.' They worshipped them, but when the first Wonderlanders arrived, they saw the truth—that the Black Towers were evil. There was a sinister presence about them—they made you sick, made you crazy, made you crave touching their sap.

"You know the rest. Eventually Wonderlanders pushed the Yurkei back into the mountains where they belonged and built Wonderland Palace and its townships. The Black Towers stand as a warning to Wonderlanders—break the law and enter the Towers. Centuries came and went, and the first set of Club Cards built the Iron Web."

"But if the wood cannot be penetrated—" Wardley began.

"Aye. It cannot be. The iron walkways are completely self-suspended. They were designed by Jackrey, the best architect that Wonderland has ever seen. All the walkways are connected, but none actually touch the towers. It's how the Clubs get from one tower to the next, from top to bottom. Unless we are inside, in which case, we are probably there for other"—he looked at Dinah; she kept her eyes on the floor—"purposes."

"And you never worry about someone escaping?"

Yoous stood and stretched. "You feel good since you've been here, boy?"

Wardley gave a defeated shrug. "I guess not, no. I feel . . ." Dinah could see him searching for the word. He cleared his throat. "Unsteady."

"That's the towers. It's inside her roots, some sort of drug that clouds the senses and confuses the mind. Most of the prisoners here are insane, but they didn't come in that way. The roots make sure of it." He rose. "I shouldn't speak any more. This prisoner needs reminding about manners."

He began unlocking Quizzer's cell door. The tiny man gave a howl and scuttled to the back of the cell, his fingers clawing his black cell wall. It dripped with slimy black moisture. "Give me the tree for the queen. Give her to me!" he howled.

Yoous slapped him down to the floor with little effort. "I'm thinking a finger or two will remind you not to touch other prisoners."

Dinah gave a shudder and without thinking, turned into Wardley's shoulder. He was smarter, and shoved her away.

"Don't touch me!" he barked.

Yoous pointed at Dinah. "Don't feel sorry for him. In a week's time you will envy him. The High Treason Tower houses the worst. Losing a few fingers will be nothing compared to what's in store for you. Now go, I need to take him down." He yanked Quizzer to his feet. *"Walk!"* he screamed.

Wardley didn't need to be told twice. He pulled Dinah's chain toward the door. "Er, thank you!" he called, unable to hide his good manners. All he heard in reply was a blood-curdling scream.

Stepping outside the Black Towers was the closest thing to heaven Dinah had ever experienced. The air was crisp and cool on her face, and she could breathe without fear of retching. There was about a two-foot gap between the doorway and the iron walkway. Wardley helped her to step over the space. That was good, thought Dinah, since she surely would fall to her death without his steady arms. Walking upon the Iron Web was just as terrifying as she had imagined from her bedroom balcony all these years. It shifted ever so slightly beneath their weight, a metal groan rising up from below them. Curling iron arched away from the tower, twisting to several different doors on each tower. The walkways went up and down the towers in gently sloping spirals that suddenly shot into open air before returning down to the ground. The structure soared up in the gaps between the towers, a walkway into the sky. Dinah vaguely remembered her childhood lessons about the Iron Web—it was made of one solid piece of iron, balanced perfectly around the towers, a maze of shortcuts from one to another.

If Dinah squinted, she could see all the way to the first tower. From here she could see that the Iron Web was covered with Clubs in their gray-and-white uniforms, going about their business. They looked like insects, scurrying down and around, moving without fear hundreds of feet in the air. Some carried paperwork, others steaming piles of unappetizing food or chamber pots. All had the same gloomy, focused looks on their faces. Dinah and Wardley watched with fascination at the ease in which they navigated the mazelike twists of the web.

"Come on. We've stood here too long. We're going to attract attention." Wardley began to lead her carefully down from the tower door. "Hurry," he said with finality.

Walking as quickly as they could while attached by chain, they stepped out onto a thin iron walkway that arched between all the towers. The ground grew farther and farther away as they followed the twisty path out into the open air between the great Black Towers, humming like hives in the unflinching winter sun. They climbed in silence. Several Clubs gave them strange looks as they passed. Wardley dripped with a nervous sweat.

Being outside the Towers gave Dinah a chance to truly look at them. The black bark was shiny on the surface—it glimmered in the sunlight. Tiny striations marked each strip as it ascended into the sky, and the outline of thickly tangled roots was barely visible. *I can see why the Yurkei would worship these*, she thought. *They are indeed "a colossal and terrible wonder."* She also had a fantastic view of Wonderland Palace from the walkway and paused to look for her apartments.

"We're almost there," breathed Wardley, jerking her back to reality. "We find Faina Baker, get our answers, and then we leave. I'm starting to feel bad about this."

Dinah attempted a smile. "You always felt bad about this."

"Don't smile," he snapped. "I'm not going to end up in here because you can't keep a smile off your silly face."

They made their way through the twisted iron until

they arrived at the Seventh Tower. They both stopped out-side the door: a wide hole in the roots that someone had fitted with steel.

"Take your last breath of clean air," Dinah whispered.

They inhaled deeply, and Wardley pushed the door open. The Seventh Tower did not smell as strong as the Murder-ers' Tower, and Dinah was grateful for that. However, there was a completely different feel in this dark spiral—it felt sin-ister, as if they had stepped into the very depths of evil. The other tower had been filled with screams and blood, whereas this one was completely silent. There was malice in the air, a hopelessness that permeated each breath. They had entered the tower closer to the bottom this time, and once their eyes adjusted to the light, Dinah quickly became aware of a hulking shadow standing behind them. She shrank behind Wardley as the shadow stepped forward.

"What business have you in the Treason Tower?" he asked, without a hint of humor or pleasantry. Dinah sud-denly missed Yoous.

Wardley yanked Dinah forward. "We were sent here by Yoous at the Murderers' Tower. We have business with the traitor Faina Baker. My prisoner is here to extract information from her."

The Card stepped into the light. His gray-and-white Club uniform was pristine and clean, a far cry from Yoous's blackened hands and clothing. This guard wore the pointed helmet of the Clubs, its black points hovering like spikes above his cheeks. There was a monstrous sword strapped to his back. Wardley, lean and muscular, suddenly looked like a scrawny child in his massive shadow.

The Club gave a nod. "You are not the first person to try and extract information from Ms. Baker. There was another one here earlier this week, slimy fellow."

Wardley cleared his throat. "Yes. That was cleared through Erinsten previously."

The man gave a grunt and began walking toward the middle of the spiral. He spun around. "You coming? I don't have all day to ferry around traitors and amateur Cards who don't know their manners."

Wardley and Dinah followed silently. Suspended from the middle of the top spire was a platform, made of the same twisted iron as the Iron Web. There was no enclosure on any of the sides so it was completely flat, aside from some gears and a lever sticking out from the middle. Wardley held fast to Dinah's chains as they jumped onto the platform. It swung in the open air, and Dinah clutched Wardley's shoulder to avoid pitching off into the void.

"You seem close to that prisoner," remarked the guard. "Are you taking your pleasure on the side? There are a few gals in the Thieves' Tower I visit weekly. At first they protested, but now they enjoy it. Takes their minds off the torture, not that it's so bad in that tower. Just a finger or toe now and then. But they don't need fingers or toes to spread their legs, do they?"

Dinah could see anger flood Wardley's face. He distracted himself by peering down to the tower floor. It was bare. "Do you not torture here?"

The guard glanced over at them with annoyance. "How familiar are you with these towers?" His eyes narrowed. "I've never heard of you."

Wardley threw him an exasperated look. "I've never heard of you either. But I'm sure Erinsten would be happy to hear of your outside pleasures in the Thieves' Tower."

Dinah could see a growing skepticism in the guard's eyes as he looked back and forth from Wardley to her. Something had to change. She plastered an insane grin on her face and without thinking, hurled herself at the guard. The platform gave a violent lurch. She managed to wrap both arms around his neck before he threw her back with tremendous force. She flew through the air and bounced off the iron, rolling to her side, just avoiding plunging into the darkness. The platform swayed and lurched. Dinah clawed at it and gave a low feral growl, letting spittle roll over her red lips. She lunged again for the guard. Wardley grabbed the chains around her wrists and flung her roughly down. Blood spurted from Dinah's elbow, a bright splash of red against the black iron. She writhed around Wardley's feet.

"Control her!" the Club Card screamed. "She's mad! She'll tip the platform!"

Wardley yanked Dinah up. His brown eyes met hers, and Dinah saw a bewildered amazement dance across his handsome face. The man looked away from them as he lumbered toward the center of the platform, grumbling to himself about Cards and whores.

"Mad, just like Faina Baker. With any luck, they'll kill each other, and we won't have to put up with this constant stream of visitors." He glowered at Wardley as he grabbed a thick metal chain that hung through the center of the platform. "Hold on to something solid."

Dinah wrapped her fingers around the decorative iron swirls on the platform. Wardley kept one hand firmly around her chain and the other around his sword hilt. The man released a loud grunt and yanked downward on the rusty lever, which was thicker than Dinah's arm. The platform gave a shudder, and suddenly they were hurtling up into the tower, chains rattling above them. Dinah saw flashes of light and the doorways to a dozen cells as they surged upward, the walls narrowing the higher they went. Iron wheels wailed against the metal chains as they neared the pulley. The guard used his foot to pull a lever that lay flush against the floor, and the platform ground to a violent halt. Nausea rushed up from Dinah's stomach, and she choked back bitter bile.

"Faina's cell is number ten/six." He eyed Dinah again. She nibbled on her knuckle and eyed him warily. "Make it quick. Once Cray releases her from the root, there's only a short time that she'll be able to speak before . . ."

"Before?" Wardley took a bold leap off the platform, dragging Dinah with him. The platform swung in the empty air.

"You'll see. I don't want to spoil the surprise. Cray! Faina has more visitors."

A scrawny boy ran out of a narrow tunnel, his feet black and bare. An old Card clasp was pinned to his ancient Card tunic. The fabric was worn so thin that Dinah could see the boy's breaths rattle his ribs. He gave them a toothless grin before bending over in front of Dinah. At first she thought he was bowing, and a rush of panic held her still, but then he began touching her boots. "Fancy boots we have here. I reckon maybe I'll get my hands on these sooner or later, if they're not snatched."

She glanced down at her wool dress and brown boots. They were lower class by her standards, but now she realized with a flush of shame that the clothing she donned to appear poor was still richer than anything this boy had ever seen. He stood and stared at her face with curiosity.

"Follow me, lass. Don't walk too close to the cells."

He gave a laugh. "'Course, you'll be seeing these cells close enough, so it probably doesn't matter if your fellow tower mates get to know you a little better."

Wardley gave the boy a stern look. "Take us to Faina, Cray."

The spiral leading upward grew tighter and tighter until Dinah felt like she was simply turning in a circle. Looking down made her dizzy, but looking up was even worse. As the pointed ceiling of the tower loomed closer and closer, the shimmery black wood brushed the top of Dinah's hood. When it seemed they could climb no farther, Cray appeared to step right into the wall. He poked his head out. "You slums coming?"

Dinah found herself led by Wardley through a slender opening in the wood. Roots twisted overhead; this part of the tower seemed to be the least solid of the structure. Every once in a while a tiny pink snowflake would find its way in through cracks in the wood. *It's so beautiful*, thought Dinah, watching it dissolve against the black ground. *Such a small beauty in such a terrible place.*

Cray pulled a huge ring of keys from the wall. "She's

just up in here. I gotta pull her off the tree."

Unlike the lower cells, this particular cell had a thick iron door, interwoven with oily black roots. Pressing out from the other side, a handprint was etched into the iron. Someone had pressed so hard and long that the image lingered on. Dinah's stomach gave a violent lurch, and the chains binding her shook and leaped. Cray stared for a moment at her hands and then turned back to the door.

"Stand near the door. It takes a few seconds to free her from the root."

Ten

It was hard to make out exactly what they were seeing in the shadowy light. Faina's cell was dark, but once Dinah's eyes adjusted, she could make out a stone slab for sleeping, a chamber pot, and a threadbare rug on the floor. From there, Dinah's eyes traveled up the wall to Faina Baker's face, all while fighting the horror rising up inside of her.

Faina was pressed against the wall, held tight by leather bonds that looped over her abdomen and chest. She writhed against them, her feet slipping in the black fluid that dripped down from above. Thin tendrils of black roots snaked out of the wall and into Faina Baker's open mouth, nose, and ears. All down her body, the black roots circled and twisted, moving slowly, leaving a thin black film as they slithered inch by inch. Dinah gripped Wardley's arm as a tendril crawled its way up Faina's face.

Faina's eyes were open, frozen in panic; a low moan came out of her mouth filled with black roots. Cray sauntered up to her and unhooked the leather straps from her torso, narrowly avoiding the roots that reached ever so slightly for his hand.

Wardley's mouth twisted with anger. "What are you doing to her? How can you allow this? What is . . . ?" He stepped forward, forgetting himself. Dinah could see he was unhinged, his hand on his sword hilt. Forgetting chivalry and honor was not an easy thing. Dinah yanked backward on her chain, and he remembered where he was. Cray untethered Faina, and she slouched forward. The roots slithered back from her body, retreating from her nose, mouth, and ears with a revolting sucking sound. Finally, the roots released, and Faina Baker crumpled like a rag doll onto the dirty floor.

"You strap her to the tower? That's the torture for high treason?"

Cray gave a filthy, toothless grin. "Aye. What could be worse than being strapped to the very source of the poison that corrupts the Towers? The roots take to the skin, and as you can tell, they love an opening. Eventually the poison seeps directly into the brain. It gives hallucinations and fevers, and some say the ability to see beyond the towers. The future and the past, and everything in between. The roots make you forget who you are, make you forget that you are human. What else could we do to these criminals that is worse than losing who they are?"

He laughed, and Dinah imagined silencing him with the flat of her palm. There was a faint outline left on the wall where Faina had been strapped, a root twisting itself back into place. An oily mist condensed in the head area.

"Make it quick," snapped Cray.

Dinah stepped forward. Faina Baker was a shred of a woman. Her arms were as thin as sticks, and thick gray veins ran the length of them. The roots left black dirt behind where they had been clinging to her face and torso, as if she had been burned. What once had been lovely blue eyes were now sunken into two dark holes that stared out of a gaunt face.

"My gods," muttered Wardley to Cray. "How can you live with yourself?"

Faina Baker was a walking skeleton. Her once-honeyed yellow hair was streaked with white, her lips dark with blood and bite marks. Faina Baker looked up at Dinah from the ground, a string of drool sneaking out of her mouth and pooling on the ground. She began singing in an eerily beautiful voice—high and lovely, her tears mingling with her warbling vibrato.

"You have a few minutes, that's all." Cray walked to the cell door.

Wardley gave Dinah a nudge forward as Cray slammed the cell door shut behind them. *I could be stuck in here forever*, thought Dinah, with a rush of panic. *I should never have come*. She knelt before Faina in the muck. The woman lay still on the ground, her fingernails tracing broken hearts in the mud.

"Hello, Faina, my name is Dinah. I don't believe we've

met before, but somehow I think you have information for me."

Faina reached out and grazed her blackened fingers down Dinah's face, leaving foul trails. Her vacant eyes looked through Dinah. "I know you," she whispered. "The queen, the queen. You aren't the queen, not yet. Keep your head."

"I am. I received a note, to come here, to find you, to talk to you. Who are you?"

Faina blinked a few times and looked directly at Dinah. A moment of clarity lit up her eyes as the black marks left by the roots faded into her skin. Her arm reached out and clutched Dinah's fingers roughly. "She's not who you think she is, she is a good girl, be merciful, please. The one you call the duchess . . ."

Vittiore? Dinah's heart skipped a beat. *This was about Vittiore?*

"Are you talking about Vittiore?"

"He came in the night. With the devil steed and many men. He was looking for something, looking for the yellow and the blue, looking for something he would never have again, something he had only once." Her voice lifted in a song. "Blond, blond like the sun on the shore she was . . ." Her eyes widened. "The wrong crown waits for her. The strings will tighten around her arms, and she will dance, oh she will dance for her head, strings around her wrists like roots. Curls in blood, curls in blood . . ."

The woman was making no sense. It reminded Dinah of every conversation she had ever had with Charles. She took Faina's hand in her own. "Please try not to speak in riddles. I need you to remember what you know."

Faina blinked. "Have you seen my baby? She was here, once, inside of me. Now there is nothing but the black, the roots. They show me things. I know things. She will find her death under the heart, trampled under the devil steed, just like me."

"She's mad!" hissed Wardley.

Faina raised her head to look at Wardley and licked her lips. "You must have been mad," she said, "or you would not have come here."

Dinah pulled Faina to her feet and rested her on the stone platform that served as her bed. "What do you know? I need you to tell me. Think. How did you get here?"

Faina's lower lip trembled and black tears that looked like ink began rolling down her face. "We did nothing but serve Wonderland, all our lives. Catching clams and oysters for the king's pleasure and table. I have seen the beauty of a fiery sunset over the Western Sea, of shells in my baby's hand. And then it was all gone, in the flash of a silver blade. All because of *you*. The queen's cold bed was for naught, but she will, oh yes, she will rise like the sun, my own little sun . . . she will possess all that you desire."

She leaned against Dinah, who held her breath against the wave of nausea that passed through her. Faina smelled like nothing she could ever describe—the smell of the tower itself, an ancient evil, filth, and death.

"Please, Your Highness! Please don't let them tie me to the tree. The root shows me things, horrible things, beautiful things . . ." She started babbling incoherently.

"That's Yurkei," hissed Wardley. "She's speaking Yurkei!"

Dinah listened closely, but all her language lessons were useless. The Yurkei that Faina was speaking was a strange blend of sounds and random words. Faina's body gave a jerk, and then another. Dinah held Faina's head gently with her hands as she thrashed in the darkness.

"I know," she murmured. "I know it hurts. I know it feels horrible to not have control."

She flashed to Charles, how his mind was a wild, unknowable thing, always seeing but never sharing, straining but always failing to make a human connection. With a loud scream, Faina's seizure ended and she laid her head on Dinah's lap. Her bright blue eyes shone with a new clarity, her voice unwavering. The madness had retreated. "You have to go," she whispered. "Straddle the devil. And when the time comes, do not open the marked door. Please!" She grabbed Dinah's arm, long nails ripping into the princess's pale skin. "Do not heed the blood of secrets."

"What do you mean?" Dinah heard the faint sound of marching from down below. The Clubs were changing their watch.

"It's time to leave, right now. We have to go!" insisted Wardley. "We will not be so lucky with the night Clubs coming in."

Dinah leaped up. "We can't leave her here like

this—they'll bind her to the tower again!"

"What did you think went on in the Towers? Tea and tarts? That isn't our choice to make! She is a prisoner here, and you are the princess. We need to leave. You won't get any more information from her!"

He was right. Faina was clawing her way toward the back of the cell. Wardley reached into his baldric and pulled out a thin dagger, barely the width of a finger. He placed it on the ground and kicked it across the floor toward Faina's blackened hand.

"What are you doing?" demanded Dinah.

"A kindness," snapped Wardley. He yanked Dinah to her feet. She tore away from him and knelt beside Faina, covering her with her cloak.

"I'll come back for you, I will," she insisted.

Faina closed her eyes. "Not this time. There will be a bloody end for Faina, no baby at her breast." She looked up at Dinah, a peaceful contentment passing over her features. "Oh, my poor queen. Your heart will sway your hand."

"*Cray!*" Wardley shouted, banging his sword against the lock. "Open this cell at once."

Cray trotted out of the darkness and unlocked it with a smile. "Did you have your way with her? She was a pretty one when she came in, not so much now that the tree has taken her for itself. . . ."

Wardley slapped him across the face with an open hand. "A true man never needs to take by force."

Cray stared at Wardley with awe as he pushed past. "I'll strap her back up now. C'mon, Faina."

"Can't you just leave her alone?" snapped Dinah.

"Nope. We are on orders from the king himself to have her strapped in from sunrise to sunset." He easily propped Faina against the wall and pulled the leather strap across her chest. Roots began to stir and pulse away from the wall.

"Even I think it's cruel. The most I've ever seen a prisoner strapped in to the tower is an hour a day. And that was for the Gray Turncoat."

The Gray Turncoat was an assassin sent by the Yurkei. He had come very close to killing the king, but his mortal fault was that he underestimated Cheshire. After his failed attempt at poisoning, he spent a month in the Towers before he lost his head, which was then sent back to the Yurkei on horseback. Cray pinched Faina's thin cheek between his grubby fingers. "This one must have done something beyond horrible, but that makes sense from what she was saying when she arrived."

Dinah took a step closer to Cray. "And what was that?" she asked, her voice low.

"It depends on what you can offer me, *Your Highness*."

Dinah recoiled as if she had been punched in the chest.

"I may have been raised in the Towers, but I'm no fool." He looped an arm around her shoulder. "I heard the princess was homely, but I have to say, you aren't homely at all. I find you quite striking. Look at that strong chin, those dangerous eyes."

Dinah heard the metallic swish of Wardley drawing his sword. Cray smiled and pointed his finger at Wardley over Dinah's shoulder. "You will never get out of these towers without me." He giggled. "Time is of the essence. The evening watch is coming in, and those Clubs are two times more brutal and suspicious. They will see through you in seconds."

Dinah clutched the amethyst ring in her dress pocket.

The stone was the size of a quail egg. She withdrew it slowly.

"I will offer you this if you tell me what Faina said when she arrived, *and* if you get us out alive. It will also buy your silence. It's worth about ten years' wages, or enough to buy a cottage in the village."

Cray's eyes lit up, the reflection of the gem flashing over his greedy pupils. "Yes. Yes, I will tell you, and make sure you get out of the Towers in one piece. But we must leave now."

He read Dinah's thoughts before she could open her mouth.

"We can't take her with us. There is no hope for her. The roots have poisoned her mind and body, and she is more of the tree than she is of this world. Besides, all prisoners deserve their just punishment."

Before Dinah could object, Wardley took her by the elbow and dragged her toward the door. Cray slammed the cell door shut after them, locking it. Dinah glanced sadly back. Faina met her eyes and for a moment she saw a peaceful look of finality pass over her features. Then she gave a whimper of pain and surrendered to the roots twisting their way across her face. A maniacal laugh escaped from her bloody mouth and followed them as they ran. Hot tears splashed down Dinah's face as she shuffled after Wardley. The chains were still clamped over her wrists, and she struggled to keep her balance while they followed Cray through one dark hall after another.

"What is the quickest way to the Iron Web?"

Cray pointed down two levels. "See that iron poker hanging there? Between those two cells, there is a door to the web."

Dinah's feet flew as they sprinted down the platforms, spiraling lower and lower. Prisoners called out from their cells, extending their blackened hands to grab at Dinah. Cray motioned to a tattered rope lying on the ground between two cells. "Follow the rope out to the Iron Web. From there, you're on your own. I have to return to Faina's cell before anyone notices I was gone."

From the corner of her eye, Dinah saw Wardley spin, his black Club cape flashing behind him. In a second, he was behind Cray, his sword pressed across Cray's pale neck.

"You will tell us what Faina said, or you will die here,

and I can assure you, no one will ever investigate how a spineless coward lost all his blood."

Cray gave a squeak. "She didn't say much, not much of nothing. It's mostly madness. When she came in, she was gagged, she was! When we took it out, she would just cry and say, 'She'll wear a crown to keep her head! She'll wear a crown to keep her head!'"

Cray began blubbering loudly. Too loudly. Wardley brought the butt of his sword down against Cray's temple, and he crumpled to the ground like an empty sack.

"Put the ring in his pocket. This is safer. He'll never want to tell someone that he was so easily overcome in his own prison or that he was bribed. Coward." Wardley spat on his face and picked up the end of the rope. Thankfully, Cray had been telling the truth, and the rope led them to a misshapen door that opened to the bright Wonderland sky. Moving as quickly as they dared without attracting attention, Dinah and Wardley navigated their way over the web back to the Murderers' Tower. Returning to the path they had arrived on required quite a bit of climbing and back-tracking; several times they ended up on an iron walkway that led to a different tower, and one time into open sky.

"A trap for escapees," mumbled Wardley as they slowly backed away from the steep drop that ended on a rocky out-cropping just inside the palace gates. "Let's not go that way again."

It took an hour, but finally they were able to find the correct path through the maze and make their way to a low door that led into the Murderers' Tower. The smell once again overpowered Dinah's senses. But this time, she didn't have time to retch. They were sprinting now, this time up the spiral, to where the forgotten door led them to the pool of ice. They could hear the marching of Clubs making their way up the spiral behind them. The next shift of Clubs was coming, and if they didn't hurry, they would have to explain themselves to an entire deck of Cards. Dinah thought of the crown in her bag. She would grab it if she needed it.

"There, there is the door!" shouted Wardley as they flew past cells and rancid chamber pots. A prisoner's hand grabbed Dinah's dress through the cell bars, and she was yanked off her feet. She hit the ground hard as the prisoner pulled her toward the cell. Dinah delivered a firm kick to the scarred hand with the heels of her boot. She jerked her dress free as the prisoner began screaming. They were almost to the door when Wardley bucked to a sudden stop and jumped sideways into a tiny slot in the wall, pulling Dinah in after him. This wasn't a doorway, rather an impossibly narrow storage chamber for clamps and chains. They could both barely fit, and Dinah found herself pressed face-first against the wall with Wardley wrapped around her.

"Yoous," whispered Wardley into her ear. "He can't see us, or we will be done for. Don't even breathe."

His warning didn't matter; Dinah couldn't. A single black root, sensing an open presence, was twisting its way up her torso, her breasts, and then onto her face. Something in the tree paralyzed her, and so she could only watch with horror as the delicate tendril reached her mouth and clawed its way inside, choking her. It sprouted a second root that started pushing into her nostrils. She wanted to cry out to Wardley, but she couldn't. Dinah was part of the tree now, and she would be forever. Visions rushed through her mind—visions of decapitated heads, white cranes, blue smoke, burning wood, pulsating mushrooms, and bright-red blood. And then she was falling, falling forward, falling into the darkness that was warm and comforting. Wardley's strong arm caught her as she pitched forward.

"Dinah? Dinah?"

She opened her eyes. She was still in the Towers, still in the slot between cells. Wardley held a broken root in his hand, his sword in the other. They watched as it twisted and writhed before turning into ash. Wardley wiped his hand on his tunic with disgust.

"The tree . . . ," she mumbled.

"You leaned against it," reprimanded Wardley. "You let it touch your skin. What were you thinking?"

Dinah shook her head. The visions were gone, already retreating back into her brain. "Yoous?" she asked as Wardley steadied her.

"He passed. We're only one level down from where we need to be. Can you walk?"

Dinah inched one foot out in front of her. "I'm fine." The longing to escape these towers of death was overwhelming. They made it to the same doorway without further trouble, and Dinah marveled at how hidden it was in plain sight, virtually indistinguishable from the roots around it. Their escape hatch waited quietly—its crooked door pouring freezing air into the damp humidity of the tower. Dinah had never seen such a welcome sight. They made their way down the stone teeth, her eyes trained on the skeleton sentry, forever frozen in the ice, forever watching the towers that held him. Dinah let her eyes play over the white holes where his eyes once were, over the gray pieces of skin crusted to the ice. She could feel the terrible vision seeping into her memory, etching its sightless stare there forever.

The thought filled her with terror as they wove their way back under the castle, sliding down the sloping tunnel they had crawled up hours before. She barely remembered the cold and the dark, Wardley leading their way with the glowing pink torch through turn after turn. They silently raced through the Great Hall, finding their way back to the cloak room without a word. It was only when Wardley started pulling off her dress did Dinah blink and realize where they were . . . and that they were safe.

Her lips trembled. "Wardley, I'm so sorry. I didn't know . . ."

"No, you didn't," Wardley snapped. "But I tried to tell you. No one can tell you anything, Dinah, not ever, because you're the princess and you do what you want. You're not unlike your father that way."

Dinah gritted her teeth. "That's not true, is it?"

"Yes. Obviously." He pulled off his filthy Card's breastplate and stuffed it into his oversack. "We're both filthy. Wipe your face and hands."

He turned away from her, and Dinah knew this conversation was over. She wiped off the dirt, layers thick, on a bright-red cloak toward the back of the room. The red reminded her of Faina's bloodstained mouth, and of her cryptic words, *She'll wear the crown to keep her head*. Pity and shame ran through her, so strong it made her tremble as she pulled on her expensive silk gown and put on her jeweled shoes, completely lost in her thoughts. The Towers were a stain on Wonderland, a bloodstain that spread out from their terrible black roots, and through the centuries the Royal Line of Hearts had used them for evil.

As she raised her hands to put her red crown back on her head, she felt her first recognition of *duty*. To be the queen meant to protect her subjects, even if it was from the practices of the royal family themselves. The Towers were Wonderland's terrible secret, a monstrosity for the entire kingdom to see and never understand. And when she was queen, she would tear them down, root by sickly root.

Her thoughts were interrupted by Wardley, his brown hair standing out in all directions, a streak of earth lingering on his cheek. Dinah lowered her head before him. "Forgive me for asking this of you. I didn't truly understand what I was asking." She licked her finger and brushed it lightly against his face, erasing the dirt from his strong cheekbone. "I will never forget what I saw today."

Wardley shook his head. "All my life I heard rumors and stories about them, but none were as terrible as—" He paused, and Dinah saw his eyes fill with tears. "We should have taken her . . . Faina."

"We couldn't," she replied simply. "We wouldn't have made it out in time, and they would have known we were there." She was learning quickly that what was right and what must happen weren't always the same thing. Dinah heard a quiet shuffling outside the door—the Cards were obviously curious about the suspected passion going on inside the cloak room.

"It's time," she said.

"You don't have the ring anymore," said Wardley. Dinah turned the handle to the cloak room door, aware that she would never again be the naive girl who entered it.

Her eyes were dark when she turned around. "I'll take care of it. I have a sapphire brooch twice its size in my chambers." Her face glowed with determination. Wardley's breath was loud behind her as the door opened, and she saw a mangled grin stretch the corners of Roxs's face.

"Enjoyed yourselves, did ya?"

Dinah cleared her throat, and his smile quickly disappeared.

Eleven

Harris was unbearable when he was determined that Dinah learn something. "No, you're late, you're late again. You keep coming in late."

Dinah angrily shoved her books off the table. They landed with a thud at Harris's feet.

"There are more important things to do than sit here and repeat verbatim the Wonders of Wonderland." She crossed her arms in a huff. "This kingdom is falling apart, and I'm looking at pictures and reciting rhymes like a child."

Harris pushed his glasses up. "What makes you say that

the kingdom is falling apart, my dear? The Line of Hearts has never been stronger. Wonderlanders love the king, and—"

Dinah interrupted him. "They don't love him. They fear him. There is a difference."

"Fear is not always a bad thing. When you are queen, you should strive for both. These are things you should think about, child. You will soon be queen."

Dinah begrudgingly helped her guardian gather the books from the floor, and she watched as he sat down across from her, his bushy white eyebrows wiggling with maddening glee. "Dinah, may I say something?"

Dinah sighed. "You may."

"Part of being a good ruler is the constant education and finesse of the mind. The past should govern how you will shape your rule. Learn from the mistakes of your predecessors, glean understanding from the history of the Royal Line of Hearts, and understand the lay of your land—and how it came to be so. Now tell me, the Wonders of Wonderland are . . ."

"The Sky Curtain, the Twisted Wood, the Ninth Sea,

Wonderland Palace, and the Yurkei Mountains."

Harris sat back, satisfied. "You know these well."

Dinah did know them well. In fact, she had been study-ing up on her land every evening as she lay in bed. In the two months that had passed since her journey into Wonderland's depraved prison system, Dinah was reading more than she ever had before, late into the night. She would do anything to keep the memories and dreams of the Black Towers away. Still, no matter how mentally exhausted she made herself, her last thoughts before sleeping would be Faina Baker's grim face as a black root twisted its way into her mouth. More often than not, her dreams were dark and demented— not unlike the Towers themselves—and she would wake drenched in sweat and flooded with panic, clawing at her own mouth.

While her learning had increased tenfold, her patience with lessons and the daily routine of the castle had ceased to exist. Suddenly she could not stand the long introductions, the formality of the court, the ridiculous routines and prac-tices that took up more than half the day. *For gods' sake*, she thought, taking a gulp of tea, *it takes me two hours or so to eat breakfast and get dressed. So much could be done in that time.*

As if he could read her thoughts, Harris began picking up the books and putting them back on the bookshelves that lined Dinah's walls. "I see Your Highness is in no mood for lessons today. Are you sure that nothing is bothering you? You have been sullen and withdrawn lately, which is not very princess-like behavior, especially with your coronation coming up in a few weeks."

Dinah simply shook her head. She could tell no one about what she had seen. This kind of news would surely kill Harris, who had slowed down in recent years. And while she trusted her twitchy tutor, she loved him too, and she would never drag him into something dark.

"Thank you, Harris. I'm just tired. And I long to begin my rule."

"Do not wish that too early, my dear. Once you begin it, you may long for your childhood days once more."

I'll never have those again, thought Dinah, *not now that I know what lingers beyond the palace.* Dinah stood up and brushed off her maroon-and-white-striped dress. "I think I'm going to visit Charles this morning. Tell the servants to pass the message along."

Harris clapped his hands. "That sounds like a brilliant idea. Please tell Lucy and Quintrell that I send my regards."

Dinah nodded absently as she fiddled with the small bird in her hair. Emily walked up behind her and clipped it firmly to the side of Dinah's head. "That looks lovely, my lady."

Dinah made a rumbling sound in her throat. No matter how much she tried, she could not bring herself to care about Wonderland fashion.

She walked briskly through the palace. Everywhere she went, her pace was now brisk, now that she had two Heart Cards trailing her every move. *This is how it feels to be queen*, she told herself, *so I better get used to it.* The *click-clack* of boots behind her reminded her with every step that she was never truly alone.

Quintrell was waiting for her outside Charles's door. "My queen!" he bowed.

"Not yet." Dinah smiled. "How is he today?" she asked.

"Strangely melancholy," he replied, relieving the Cards and ushering Dinah inside. "This last week he has not been himself. His mood is one of despair, and most of the time Lucy finds him weeping in corners or screaming at the walls. He seems fascinated with stars and shadows, though his work has been focused solely on the concept of shadows, all black and shades of gray. It's hard for us to see him this way. It has resulted in some of the most beautiful hats I've ever seen, though." He let out a defeated sigh. "The Mad Hatter has never been more exceptional in his talent, but our Charles is strangely detached."

Dinah rested her hand on his shoulder. "Thank you for telling me. I'm so grateful that Charles has such loving servants."

"Wait until you see what he has made for your coronation."

One month, thought Dinah. *Only one more month until I will rule beside my father.*

Charles's crooked quarters were more disarrayed than normal. Dinah waded through ankle-deep hats to reach the stairwell on which Charles precariously sat. One leg dangled off into nothing, and he seemed intensely focused on a tooth he held in one hand. Dinah winced.

"Hello, Charles. Is that your tooth?"

Charles blinked several times, his green eye staring at her while his blue one wandered to the right. His mouth was bloody. She gently wiped his lips with the sleeve of her dress as he grinned at her. "Two tooths too many to bite."

She shook her head. He leaped up, and Dinah steadied herself on a twisted wicker railing that looped overhead.

With wide eyes, he stared at her. "Do you know what the whispering mountains cry? They scream for their freedom! Then it's good night, good night, good night, all of Wonderland in a steaming pile." Charles flung his tooth off the ledge and danced down the stairs ahead of her. As they reached the bottom, his face went from enchantment to hysterics. "Tooth! I need it, I need it, fiddle dee, tooth for tooth!" He began to search frantically in a pile of hats, which flew overhead as he tunneled beneath them.

"It's here, Charles." Dinah had seen the tooth land on a pile of spotted teal feathers. She plucked it up and scrubbed it with a piece of sunrise-colored silk. He snatched it out of her hand and held it up to the light. "Ivory. Bone. Black on black texture with the teeth of different animals. A hat for a horde. A hat for a"—he did a little jig—"a warrior! A man that carried heads in a bag!"

He wrapped his hand around Dinah's. It surprised her a little. Charles reluctantly let her touch him sometimes, but he was never the instigator. His mismatched eyes looked up into hers. "Come and see. Come and see," he whispered, repeating the phrase over and over. He led her under the maze of staircases into a small back room. This was where he usually stored buttons of every size and make, but the room had been cleared, and it was empty. *Empty except for a crown.*

It sat on a wooden stool, and an open window filtered in just enough light so that it glittered and shimmered in the sun. Dinah felt the air whoosh out of her lungs. It was magnificent, a work of art of the highest order, unlike anything she had ever seen. The thick base was of brushed silver, inlaid with thousands of tiny white diamonds, all in the shape of hearts. Individual tree branches rose up from the hearts, leaping and twisting into a solid second circle that finished the top of the crown. The detail became more incredible the closer Dinah looked. The branches, when inspected, were patterned into tiny faces, their flowered mouths open in a scream. Stars, flickering in the light, hung from thin bands of silver among the creeping branches. Four Card symbols connected the vines from the sides of the crown to the top, where a diamond heart inlaid with a bird in flight sparkled in the light. The heart, she could see, had been cut in half and reassembled so it sat a tiny bit askew.

She was speechless. Its beauty was not only ten times that of her crown; it was ten times that of her father's crown. Nothing like this had been made in Wonderland, not ever. It was the most astonishing crown she had ever seen, truly a combination of art and extraordinary skill. It blazed in the sunlight.

"Charles . . . I cannot accept this. This is . . ."

She looked over at her brother. He was still, for once, watching her with puzzling sadness. She gave him a kiss on the forehead. He made a face.

"Thank you. I shall wear it every day when I am queen." Her own crown, a tiny ring of rubies, now seemed sad and pathetic by comparison. She reached out to touch the diamond heart.

"No!" Charles screamed, throwing himself on the floor,

where he began flailing. His body gave a jerk and a spasm rippled up his legs. Dinah knelt on the floor next to him, wrapping her arms around his painfully thin frame.

"Charles, breathe. Charles, calm down. I won't touch it—not yet."

She shouted for Lucy, and Quintrell flew around the corner. His face dissolved into fear for the little prince. "Hold him tight. Here, put this in his mouth." He gave Dinah a stick of hard wood. "I don't want him to bite off his tongue."

Dinah gently placed the stick into Charles's mouth and held him until the seizure passed. His body went slack in Dinah's arms, still and quiet.

"I've got him," she told Quintrell.

He gave her a gentle smile. "What do you think of your crown?"

Dinah looked back at it. It was no less beautiful from below. "I can't believe he made that. I knew he did metal and gemstone work sometimes, but this . . ."

"He's been working on it for years," Quintrell whispered. "We never wanted to spoil the surprise. The day it graces your head will be a glorious day for us, for Charles, for Wonderland. I have faith that you will be a great queen."

Dinah looked down at her tiny brother, his limbs quivering under her hands. Her arm was heavy under his shuddering spine. *Two broken children*, she thought, *waiting for a mother who will never return*. She looked into Charles's eyes and stroked his hair. "The crown should have gone on his head," she replied. "If he weren't mad, Charles would have been the heir, the King of Hearts."

Quintrell dropped his huge hand against her black hair. "It was never meant to be, Your Highness. Shall I take him from you?"

Dinah shook her head. "No, I'll stay. Would you mind bringing me some pillows?"

Charles's small mouth opened and shut as his eyes flickered beneath pale eyelids. Dreaming of hats, she prayed. Hats and trees and tarts. She snuggled in beside him, his greasy head resting against her shoulder. They rested together, brother and sister—Charles finally sleeping soundly after his seizure ended, and Dinah staring in wonder at the crown, watching how the changing light played over its features. She stayed with him for a few hours until Lucy stepped into the room, tucking in her lacy apron.

"Dinah, Charles should be put into his bed now. Quintrell can carry him there. After his seizures, he sleeps for about two days. It's the most sleep he ever gets, so we take advantage of it and attempt to categorize and clean his materials and living space." She looked at the small, empty room. "At least we don't have to clean this room anymore."

Dinah carefully shifted Charles off her hip and let Quintrell take him. Charles was so thin Quintrell could cradle him like a child.

"I'll come back later this week," said Dinah, sliding her feet back into her jeweled slippers. She bent over Charles and kissed his forehead lightly, lingering on his smell of unwashed skin, sun, and fabric. "I'll see you soon," she whispered. On her way out, she stole another glance at the crown. The afternoon sun was heavy, and the rays of Wonderland's beaming light rippled across the jeweled surface. *I'll be back for you*, she thought.

Dinah walked swiftly down the stone hallway that wound around the Royal Apartments. A poof of a white bird was following her. These petite, perfectly beaked creatures ran rampant around the castle. Dinah turned and scooped it up in her hands. The bird gave a surprised squawk and then nuzzled against her ribs. Dinah let her fingers lightly play over its downy-soft feathers as she walked. Her mind wandered and jumped, replaying all that Faina Baker had said and done. It wasn't hard. Dinah wouldn't forget what she had seen and heard in the Black Towers, not ever—Faina's sunken beauty, Cray's scheming boyishness, Yoous's lazy brutality. Wardley hadn't spoken to Dinah since then, and Dinah was afraid of what he might say when he did. Surely, he resented her for dragging him there, to a place of nightmares.

Her mind kept wrapping and unwrapping itself around Faina's words. *She'll wear the crown to keep her head.* She had obviously been talking about Dinah. But why would she lose her head? No one would dare kill a royal, unless it was a Yurkei assassin, or a family next in line to the throne, but her father had all but eradicated those.

He came on a devil steed, looking for something he would never have again. That didn't make sense either. Faina had talked of the sea, but her father had battled the Yurkei tribes in the east, up against the mountains. That was where he had found Vittiore. And Cheshire, the whisperer of secrets—he was tied up in this as well, not that that was a surprise. Dinah had always loathed him, but now she had even more reason to make sure that her first days as the Queen of Hearts were his last as the king's adviser.

The bird gave another loud squawk and turned over in Dinah's hands. She looked around in surprise. She had been wandering for a while, lost in her thoughts. She was now on the king's end of the castle—the west-side Royal Apartments. Dinah rarely ventured here, for fear of running into her father. She glanced back. Her Heart Cards were behind her, looking bored and annoyed that she had wandered so long. She began walking again. *Let them follow*, she thought. *That's their job.* The late-afternoon light bathed the castle in a lovely golden glow. Her eyes lifted to a red stained-glass window, wall-sized and made of hundreds of tiny hearts. When the sun rippled through fat clouds outside, the heart appeared to be alive, a beating organ with a thousand moving parts. She sighed. Wonderland Palace was so beautiful, so ancient. Sometimes she forgot how lovely it was, how much she loved it.

"Dinah?"

The sound was so soft it made her jump. She dropped the bird. It gave Dinah an angry peck on her shin before scuttling down the hall. Vittiore stood behind her, a layered peach gown on her thin frame. Her blond curls were pulled to one side and clipped with a pale-pink rose. Her two lady's maids flanked her sides, as they always did. They wore matching dresses—red-and-white stripes with blue piping, like frosting on a cake. They were identical twins, born of a Mrs. Dee, a striking lady of the court who stood in high favor—too high, Dinah suspected—with the king.

Dinah's eyes narrowed. "That rose clip was my mother's."

Vittiore raised a flustered hand to her head. "I'm sorry, I didn't . . ."

Palma, the quieter of the twins, stepped forward. "What the duchess wears is no business of yours." She gave a silly giggle that made Dinah grind her teeth together. "It's not like you care about the fashion of Wonderland. Your mother had much better sense than you ever will."

Nanda, her second lady-in-waiting and the meaner twin, let out a derisive laugh. "Don't blame the princess—it's not her fault. Emily has no sense how to dress people, or what a lady should wear. She's of common birth. It's well-known."

Dinah clenched her teeth. "Do not speak of Emily. She is a loyal servant and a more than suitable maidservant. I require more of my servants than simply dressing me like an overstuffed bird."

Palma narrowed her eyes. "Emily is not as loyal as you think."

"Quiet, Palma," snapped Nanda.

"Both of you, shush now. You forget your place," Vittiore ordered quietly. "Go back to my chambers and prepare some thistle tea for the princess and me. Now."

Palma and Nanda gave an irritated bow and scampered off toward Vittiore's chambers, their steps perfectly in sync. Dinah placed her hands on the hips of her striped gown, suddenly feeling very plain. "I have no desire for tea. I give you permission to enjoy it with your gossipy and useless maidservants. Good-bye." She turned to go.

"No, wait. Just one cup."

Dinah tilted her head and stared at her half sister, the Duchess of Wonderland. They had never been together without the king, not once since Vittiore had arrived. Dinah avoided Vittiore at all costs, and she had assumed Vittiore had done the same. They were never scheduled for the same activities, the same meals or lessons. She saw her occasionally for royal balls, croquet games, and more tedious matters of Wonderland, such as council meetings, but that was just a few times a year. During those times, Vittiore looked equally bored as Dinah, only with a hint of fear. She had always been slight and lovely, which made the much-more-solid Dinah feel like a clumsy giant around her, even here in this cavernous hallway.

Vittiore gestured again behind her. "Please, Your Highness. Just one cup with me. I apologize for Nanda and Palma. I promise the view from my balcony is quite picturesque."

When a blunt rejection alighted on her tongue, Dinah reluctantly bit it back. Perhaps she could glean some understanding of what Faina Baker was mumbling about from speaking with Vittiore. She obviously had secrets to hide.

Faina's ramblings were still steeped in mystery and cryptic madness. They remained a dark puzzle. She would have to be creative to decipher their meaning. "I will have one cup of tea."

Vittiore tripped over the edges of her gown as she turned around. "Oof! These are always too long. I can lead you there."

"I am well aware of where your apartments are," Dinah snapped. "They were my mother's." They walked in silence, the heavy steps of the Heart Cards clanking behind them.

"It's a lovely day outside, is it not? I am glad to see that spring is finally here," whispered Vittiore.

"I prefer winter," Dinah replied curtly. "I relish the frozen air blowing in from the Todren."

Vittiore's curls gave a slight shudder as she pushed open the door to her apartments. The stone hallway opened up into a bright, beautiful room. Vittiore's windows faced the Western Slope, which eventually reached the sea. Several small towns inside Wonderland proper could be seen from her window. Dinah quietly marveled at how different Vittiore's room was from hers. Dinah's apartment was filled from floor to ceiling with bookshelves. It was large and decorated with ancient treasures—globes and tiny ship models, but it would never be called lovely. It was designed for a man, for the heir her father once dreamed he would have.

Vittiore's room was the very definition of lovely. It was airy and light, very different from when Dinah had seen it last, when everything was dark and draped with black fabric, a sign of mourning for her mother. Now, gossamer pastel fabrics draped the walls, moving slightly in the breeze. Every piece of furniture was painted a pale blue, and her upholstery was a swirl of bright, pretty colors. A white peacock strutted proudly across the room, pecking at Dinah's feet. Vittiore scooped him up.

"This is Gryphon." She petted the bird's head. He gave a happy shiver. "My tea room is over here, by the window."

Her rose tea table was tiny, Dinah noted. She barely had enough room to sit across from Vittiore without their elbows touching. *She must always have tea alone*, she thought, thankful that her own tea table was large enough to fit Harris and Emily alongside her. Palma and Nanda hovered over the table, watching Dinah's every move with their meticulously painted eyes and dramatically arched brows.

Vittiore noticed Dinah's frown as Palma set down a clear-glass teacup. "I think the princess and I will have tea privately. Leave us."

"But, Your Grace, should the water run out, or the tarts need replenishing, how will we hear you? I really think it best we stay."

Dinah could see from the interaction that Vittiore had little control over her maidservants—it was more the other way around. She seemed to fear them. Dinah wasn't surprised. The Dee family was made up of relentless social climbers, their loyalty shifting with the wind.

Dinah snapped her fingers. "Leave us *now*. If you will not listen to the duchess, you will listen to me, your future queen. Make haste."

Palma curtsied and left the room with a loud sigh.

"I'm sorry. They are very protective of me," Vittiore apologized.

"It is not my concern." Dinah shrugged.

There were a few moments of silence. Dinah looked at her cup. Since the steaming water had been poured over the prickly purple flower, one of its side petals had unfurled, filling half the cup with a strange glow. A tiny stream of red liquid now poured forth from the center of the flower, which tinted the cup and the water crimson.

"What is this? I've never seen this tea flower."

Vittiore brought the cup to her lips and blew. "It's called a blood thistle. It's a wild shrub that grows out there, on the Western Slope." She nodded her head to the window. "It makes the most wonderful tea."

Dinah raised the cup to her lips. *Please don't be poison*, she thought as she took a timid sip. The tea was delicious—a heavy citrus flavor danced across her tongue before it began to buzz with an earthy aftertaste.

"It is wonderful," Dinah reluctantly agreed. She sipped the tea again with casual ease. "Do you know a woman who goes by the name Faina Baker?"

Vittiore choked on her tea and dropped her cup, which exploded against the plate. Bloodred tea splashed over the collar of her peach dress, the red spreading from fold to fold. Vittiore sputtered. "Oh, I'm so clumsy. I'm sorry. My hands have always had a shake." She began to wipe up the tea on the table. Dinah added her napkin to the effort. "No, no. I've never heard that name. Why do you ask?"

Dinah decided to be shrewd. "It's just a name I overheard."

Vittiore's already-pale skin had turned a pasty shade of white, but she seemed to have regained her composure. "It is a sadness. I pray for all those imprisoned in the Black Towers, especially women."

Dinah arched her eyebrow. She had never mentioned the Black Towers or the fact that Faina was a prisoner there. Vittiore was obviously unhinged. Behind Dinah, a door shut as Nanda left the room. She had been quietly listening.

Dinah stirred some sugar into her tea. "Tell me again where you grew up? I don't think we've ever actually spoken since your"—she paused—"arrival on our doorstep."

Vittiore took a deep breath. Her eyes looked to the left. "I was born just inside the Twisted Wood, at the base of the Yurkei Mountains. I was born in the early autumn. Your father had camped at our village during his great battle with the Yurkei and met my mother. They fell into lust."

"While he was still married. To my mother, the queen."

Vittiore blinked. "Yes. I'm sorry, I forget that sometimes. It was not right of him to be unfaithful to your
mother. I believe he was simply seeking emotional comfort
in my mother's arms, nothing more."

"And your mother?" asked Dinah.

Vittiore's eyes filled with tears. "She was a wonderful
woman. Her body matched her nature—soft and tender. By
the time I was brought here when I was fifteen, my mother
was long dead." Her voice caught in her throat. Dinah waited
patiently for her to finish. "I am so blessed to have such a
loving and gracious father, and so happy to be included in
the Royal Line of Hearts. For even though my mother was
common born, our father is a great king."

"Indeed," muttered Dinah, her mind churning. "Do
you miss the Yurkei Mountains?"

"Sometimes. They were so large, a permanent shadow
over our village. However, I am glad to be here now, in this
lovely palace." Her hand shook. "Although, to be honest, it
can be lonely. I visit your brother often."

Dinah couldn't hide her shock. Quintrell and Lucy
had never mentioned anything about Vittiore visiting. She

brought her cup down with a *clink*—the saucer underneath it cracked. "I was not aware of that. What reason could you possibly have to visit my brother?"

"There is an innocence about Charles that puts me at ease. He's mad, but he's also genuine." She gazed out the window. "He's so unlike anyone else in this palace. Charles has no motives or politics. His world is one of wonder, something that being a part of the royal family doesn't usually grant."

You aren't part of the royal family, thought Dinah. *Not really.*

"Do you miss your mother?" Vittiore inquired.

It seemed to Dinah that all the air was sucked out of the room at once. She was never asked about her mother. After the queen died, it was as if her mother had never existed. Only Harris mentioned her from time to time. Dinah found herself unable to produce a hateful reply, not about this. "I think about her smile. I think about the way she would smile to herself as she made her jeweled slippers. I remember how she would read stories to us, with different voices and accents. And how she would hold Charles—so fiercely, unlike everyone else, who held him as if he were made of glass."

Tears gathered at the corners of Vittiore's eyes. Her unflinching blue gaze unnerved Dinah, who found a fury rising inside. "Why would you ask about my mother? She was nothing to you, and she never even knew you existed. You should be thankful that she is dead, otherwise you would never have been allowed to come here, to be given everything from my father, simply out of pity for his bastard child."

Vittiore refused to rise to Dinah's taunt and changed the subject. "I can see how that would be upsetting for you. It's truly unfair." She sighed and rose from her seat, her features vacant. Her mind was obviously somewhere else as she stared at the view from her balcony. "Have you ever been outside the palace? There is a beauty you cannot dream of."

"I have no desire to leave," replied Dinah. "This is my home, my kingdom, my palace. I need to stay here."

Vittiore looked around the room anxiously. Dinah turned her head. There was no one here—what was she looking at? Dinah turned her head back and was startled to find Vittiore inches from her face. She pulled Dinah close. Their lips were almost touching, and she could feel Vittiore's flowery breath against her mouth.

"You should leave. Just go, as soon as you can," whispered Vittiore with breathless urgency. "There are things you could never understand happening here. I don't understand them either, but I hear the whispers."

"I understand you want my crown," hissed Dinah. "Isn't that what this is?"

A look of pure confusion crossed Vittiore's face. "What?"

Both girls jumped back from each other as a loud crack came from outside the doorway. It burst open and the King of Hearts strode in, a furious look upon his flushed face. He was followed by six Heart Cards, Nanda, and Palma.

"Dinah!" he thundered. "What are you doing in Vittiore's chambers?"

"We were just having tea," Dinah stammered, suddenly feeling very small.

"Are you not supposed to be at your lessons right now?"

Dinah stood shakily. Her legs gave a tremble, as they

always did in the presence of her father. *Be strong*, she told herself. *You will be queen soon.*

"I finished my lessons early. I visited Charles this morning. Apparently Vittiore has been visiting Charles as well. May I ask the last time you saw your son?"

Her father moved across the room with alarming speed, his huge hand gripping Dinah's arm. He turned his hand roughly, and Dinah's skin burned beneath it.

"Insolent child! Don't presume to have the right to lecture me on how to deal with my family. I'll see your mad brother when Wonderland has a peaceful, perfect day, with no need of a ruler."

Dinah twisted her arm from his grasp and spun to face him. "Soon you'll have much more time on your hands, when I take the throne beside you. I'll see to it that your afternoons are much more leisurely."

Before the king brought his closed hand across her face, Dinah saw a glimmer of pride in her father's eyes. She was fiercer than he realized. But it was only for a moment, and then she was sprawled on the ground, the left side of her face throbbing.

"Father, *stop!*" cried Vittiore, her blue eyes wide with shock. The King of Hearts gave her a murderous look.

"Darling, please go back to tea. Nanda and Palma will help you. Dinah, get up and go back to your apartments. Do not come here again. You can have no purpose here, besides distracting Vittiore from her studies. It is so like you to serve as a stumbling block for all good things." The king curled his fingers and two Heart Cards approached. He motioned to Dinah, and they yanked her roughly to her feet. "Take them both away."

Nanda and Palma escorted the shaking Vittiore into her dressing room, cooing gently in her ear. The king pointed to Dinah, who had pushed off the guards and was standing shakily on her own feet.

"I'm sure the princess has much to do before her coronation. Please see to it that she is placed in Harris's care, and remind him that he is tasked with keeping her in line." That was a threat, Dinah noted, not a request. The king bent over so he could peer into Dinah's black eyes. "I would hate for something to happen to Harris if he wasn't doing a good job of properly raising the future queen. Perhaps one of my own men would be better suited for the task."

Dinah's mouth gave a quiver. "*No*. No, I will stay away from Vittiore, as I always have. I have no desire to be in the presence of a bastard."

Dinah expected to feel the king's hand across her face again, but instead he gave a wicked chuckle. "Your fire impresses me, child. Always has. Stay in your part of the castle. Prepare for the coronation. I will see you on Execution Day."

The king spun around, his red cloak circling behind him—a garish bright spot in Vittiore's soft room. Dinah composed herself and took a last gaze outside Vittiore's windows as the Cards marched her to the doors. The sun was settling now, and the Wonderland sky was a ribbon of bright oranges, their lines stretching out onto the horizon. Bright-pink garden roses had begun to bloom on her balcony trellis, and outside, the last bits of pink snow sparkled in the waning light. Together, they turned the world into a blazing mix of fire and light.

Dinah sighed as a Heart Card motioned to the door. *I'm no closer to the truth than I ever was before*, she thought, *but at least I know without a doubt that Vittiore is connected to Faina.* On the ceiling above, painted silver stars sparkled in the dimming light. *It's so peaceful in here*, she thought. A *lovely bed for such a pretty liar.*

Pink snow was just a memory a month later, when Dinah stood on the muddy ground awaiting the start of the executions. Execution Day came twice a year to Wonderland. The courtyard was filled with thousands of townspeople and members of the court. Cards strolled up and down the aisles, their swords a not-so-subtle reminder to keep the peace. Two lines of Spades clad in their black uniforms put distance between the royals and the common folk. Red heart banners blossomed out from the platform, snapping in the warm spring breeze.

Execution Day used to be one of her favorite holidays—but that was before she was old enough to understand it. The rules of Wonderland decreed that a child couldn't witness an Execution Day until he or she was ten years old. Until then, it was just a lavish day filled with gifts and celebrations—a reprieve from her constant lessons. Dinah and Wardley would sneak away from the kitchen with a plate of warm tarts, sticky jam on their fingers, sugar on their noses, and gorge themselves until they were sick. When she turned ten and her father ordered her to go to the executions, Dinah was in shock for days. She had lost her mother that year, and seeing death so vivid and real had left her with many sleepless nights and bouts of hysterical crying. There were no more tarts, no more tracing patterns in the sugar on Wardley's cheek.

The more executions she witnessed, the harder her heart had become. Now, she didn't even flinch as the heads dropped neatly from their shoulders onto the white porcelain slab, a fact she was oddly proud of. A queen should have a strong stomach for justice, she reasoned. Dinah stood perfectly still now beside Harris, her face free of emotion as her terrible father made his way up to the platform. A silence fell over the noisy crowd as the entire kingdom bowed before its king, who was donning his impregnable armor, making him look like a bear, a force to be reckoned with. A black heart etched across his huge silver breastplate stood out proudly on his chest, his heavy gold crown shining in the afternoon light.

The king climbed the stairs, but not before his eyes met Dinah's. There was a strange exchange between them—he shot her a satisfied smile and Dinah, confused and unable to control her mouth, gave half a smile back. *What just happened*, she worried. She couldn't remember her father smiling at her—ever. He lumbered up the stairs, his iron footsteps echoing across the courtyard.

Heart Cards clustered in a messy line at the front of the stage, their swords clutched tightly against their chests. Her father began his customary speech, declaring the guilt of the prisoners and the great honor they bestowed upon Wonderland by allowing the kingdom to take their heads, thus clearing out the evil that lurked in Wonderland's darkest hearts. It was a gift to all the people of Wonderland, given really by him, the king. The prisoners were those chosen specifically by the Clubs for their heinous crimes, their lack of remorse, or their general level of uselessness to the kingdom. Most were murderers, some were men who had stolen money or goods, and some were women who sold themselves to men for the highest price. All were housed in the Black Towers. *That was punishment enough*, thought Dinah. *Worse than any that these naive people could ever imagine.*

Today's bunch, he announced, was made up of fourteen prisoners—nine men and five women. The list of beheadings went back several years, as there were plenty of people in Wonderland who had earned the blade. Dinah fidgeted nervously as her father read on until she felt Harris's elbow deep in her ribs.

"Stand still, child!"

She focused her attention on Wardley, who stood at the front of the stage, alongside his fellow Heart Cards. His curly brown hair had been shorn neat and tight against his head, a change that Dinah mourned each time she saw him. He looked so different, so unlike the boy she adored, so like the man he would become. Even now he stood out among the other Cards, his strong chin pointed to the side, his eyes trained on the king. He was confident and easy, the kind of man who could lead an army and slay the hearts of women with the greatest of ease.

Dinah looked at his right hand and saw two of his fingers crossing and uncrossing, a habit he had when he was nervous. An adoring smile drew up the corners of her mouth. Someday, she hoped, he would be her king, and lead beside her. Strong and compassionate, they would lead Wonderland into a new age, starting with the destruction of the Black Towers. Dinah clenched her fist. *Root by root*, she told herself. *It will be done.* Wardley glanced in her direction, and she gave him a small smile. He acknowledged it with a quick wink. Her heart gave a happy jump.

The king was finally on the platform now, looking out at the sea of red. Everyone wore red to Execution Day. Dinah reasoned that blood wasn't as shocking when everyone was already covered in crimson. Her father settled his large girth on the makeshift iron throne. A Club Card approached him with a rolled sheet of paper. After the king picked it up, he nodded and turned to address the crowd. Her father unrolled the document, and in his booming cadence he began to read the names of the condemned. Each prisoner was brought forward when his or her name was called; collectively, they took their place on the long black block, resting their heads on the stained marble.

"Jasper Che-guffe. Robinson Thomas. Abbie Tibbs. Gayleen Skinner. Earthe Hicket. Faina Baker."

Dinah's head jerked up. *No, no, no, no . . .*

Her father continued reading the names, but Dinah's vision had tunneled onto the tiny blond woman who was being dragged to the block. Surprisingly, she looked much better than she had in the towers—her dirty blond hair was still caked with grease and her thin arms were covered in bruises, but the madness in her eyes had retreated, and she had obviously been eating, as she had put on some weight. *They took her off the tree*, Dinah realized. *That's what is different. They fattened her up to make her look like a normal prisoner before the crowds.*

Faina strained against her chain, forcing a Club Card to drag her toward the block. Her mouth was torn, and it was no wonder, considering the metal gag that was wrapped around her face and shoved between her bloodied lips. She struggled in vain, trying desperately to cry out, her eyes trained on the royal family. The Card leading her gave a hard yank on the chain, and Faina was jerked forward to her knees before the long white block. Dinah clenched and unclenched her hands. Her body felt like she had been suddenly plunged into icy waters. She couldn't take her eyes off Faina. What could she do?

Faina gave a muffled sob and tried crawling toward the front of the platform, where Heart Cards with swords waited patiently for her. Her watery eyes were fixed on Dinah as the Cards pushed her back toward the block. A Club Card yanked her up by her hair.

"Feisty!" the king yelled, and the crowd laughed with him. Through her metal gag, faint gurgling screams could be heard. Dinah was seized with panic. Should she try to stop this? What reason could she possibly give? She looked toward Wardley. He was pale and shaken, staring at Faina as the guard slapped her down and held her head against the block, leaning on her cheek with all his strength.

Dinah grabbed Harris's red cloak. "I'd like to grant

mercy to that woman, the small one."

Harris looked back at her with alarm. "Why? Do you know the woman?"

Dinah shook her head. "No. Look at her, Harris. Does she look like a criminal?"

Harris shook his head. "Didn't you listen to the charges? That woman murdered a Club squire in the towers just last week, a young boy."

The knife, oh gods. Dinah was talking fast, frenzied. "But the waiting list for Execution Day goes back about three years, does it not?"

Harris wrapped his chubby arm fast around Dinah's waist and brought his mouth to her dark hair. "Do not upset the king, my child. Mercy is only his to give on Execution Day, and you do not want him to see you as trying to take the throne early. There is nothing you can do. She is on the block for murder, and I have no doubt that her crime was horrible. Otherwise she would not be here. Only the worst criminals are executed, and the Clubs must have good reason to grant them death. Trust in the king's justice. One day, when you are queen, you can grant mercy to whomever you chose."

Dinah angrily pushed him away. "This is not justice," she snapped.

She felt trapped, a cat in a cage, watching Faina Baker's dirty blond hair spill over the white marble. Faina was weeping and choking on her gag, and she kept throwing her arms out in front of her, as if she was trying to embrace the crowd. The crowd, in turn, murmured its approval. They loved a good show, and this madwoman determined not to die was giving them one. She had the look of a crazed beast, her desperation palpable and real. Dinah took a step toward the king before Harris locked his hand around her arm.

"Do not. You put us all at risk."

Dinah stopped. He was right. She could not risk angering the king so close to her coronation. Her father caught her commotion with Harris from the corner of his eye. He raised his Heartsword in Dinah's direction and then pointed it toward Faina. It was a quick, subtle movement, but Dinah understood instantly.

This was her punishment. *He knew, oh gods, he knew.* He knew they had been in the Black Towers, knew that Dinah had talked to her.

Faina twisted and writhed against her chains, her eyes never leaving the front row. The king picked up his Heartsword and walked the line of prisoners, taking in each one and looking into their eyes. He stopped in front of Faina, said something quiet in her ear, and continued on. After he had walked up and down the long white block, he motioned to the Club Card. The crowd stirred. This was the moment they had been waiting for, and no doubt money had exchanged quick hands after the prisoners were led out. Betting on the king's mercy was a common practice. The Card walked forward and cleared his throat.

"The king, in all his glory and righteousness, has decided to give mercy this day. These prisoners that lay their heads on the block are blessed, chosen to exemplify the justice of Wonderland, the Black Towers, the Club Cards, and the Royal Line of Hearts. Because of his generous nature, the king chooses one prisoner for mercy every Execution Day. This year, the king's mercy is given to one Robinson

Thomas, for his crime of theft."

A thundering cheer rose up from those peasants who had bet on Thomas. A handsome redheaded man clothed in rags was unchained from the line and led away, but not before he fell at the king's feet, weeping and trailing his mouth over the king's boots. Dinah knew what would happen to him after he left: he would be fed and bathed and then trained as a Spade, trained to fight, to kill. As Robinson left the platform, the buzzing of the crowd grew deafening.

"Off with their heads!" screamed out a shrill voice from the back of the courtyard. "Off with their heads, off with their heads!" the crowd echoed, growing louder and louder, until the very ground rumbled with the sound.

The king motioned with his Heartsword, and the executioner stepped forward. Dinah closed her eyes for a split second, telling herself what she always did on the day of execution. That life was just like this: given and taken, and that these were criminals who deserved their sentence. She would not be like the common people who relished the fall of the ax, the rush of red blood. But she wouldn't be like the high-born ladies either, who turned away into their handkerchiefs with a whimpering sigh. She was her father's daughter, who did not shy from the consequences of this life. Blood was just blood.

But as she opened her eyes again, she only saw Faina. She had stopped struggling and stared openly at the crowd now, a peaceful calm coming over her face as tears dripped down her cheeks and onto the marble block. She had come to terms with her death. The other prisoners weren't faring so well, as they screamed or prayed. Dinah felt her own tears leaking from her eyes, and wiped them quickly with her red cloak. *My father will not see my tears*, she thought. *I will not give him what he wants this day.* A fury raged in her chest, hot as flame.

The headsman raised his double-weighted sword, and the first head fell. Then the second. On and on down the line, until the sword hovered above Faina. Dark blood dripped off the blade onto her pale face, a black tear mingling with her own.

I'll truly never know, thought Dinah. *I'll never know the reason I ate a piece of paper with her name on it. She didn't tell me enough. The Towers took my answers.*

Faina smiled at Dinah, and for a moment, Dinah saw how stunningly beautiful she must have been, once upon a time. The blade came down with a whoosh, and Faina's head dropped swiftly away from her body. A crimson waterfall now covered the block where her head had been seconds before. Dinah didn't have time to react because of the movement on her right. Vittiore had fainted, pitching face-first into the mud on the other side of Harris, landing with a violent thud.

Dinah watched in stunned silence until she realized what was happening, and then took a few steps and knelt beside her, attempting to turn her over. Her body flapped back against Dinah. The crowd gasped. Even though Vittiore was light, her dead weight was almost too much. With a groan, Dinah turned her over, sinking knee-deep into the mud, Vittiore splayed dramatically across her lap, her white dress settling all around Dinah like swirling waves. Nanda and Palma were circling around her like dumb birds, crying and screaming but not actually doing anything.

Dinah looked down at the duchess. Anger rushed through her at having Vittiore so near—a pale-pink cheek against her forearm, blond curls crushed under her bosom, but she still held on. The royal family could not seem fractured, even when its foundation was cracked. Mud had somehow covered exactly half of Vittiore's perfect face, which was porcelain white. Her normally coral lips were red with blood—she had been biting them. Dinah remembered then that Vittiore had never been to Execution Day. She had never seen the heads roll, something Dinah had witnessed many times.

She noticed movement out of the corner of her eye: Wardley was rushing down upon her to aid Vittiore, and the rest of the Heart Cards were following his lead. Spectators and lords were raising their hands in concern for the duchess, and the crowd watched them both with rapt fascination. *This is a gruesome display*, she thought. *The bright rose of Wonderland being held by the dark thorn who would be queen.*

Dinah brought her open palm down hard across Vittiore's face. "Wake up, bastard."

Vittiore's clear blue eyes opened, and she gasped. "Dinah?" she stuttered, sounding even more pathetic than she looked. "He promised, he promised . . ." Her eyes met

Dinah's with a direct gaze. "I will wear the crown to keep her head."

Then she was out cold again. Dinah let her fall back into the mud with a thud. Suddenly everyone was on top of them. Vittiore was yanked away from Dinah by Wardley, who cradled her like a child and carried her back to the castle, followed by Palma, Nanda, and a dozen Heart Cards.

Harris helped Dinah to her feet. "My lady, that was most certainly brave and giving of you."

Harris seemed delighted at Dinah's unexpected comforting of Vittiore. He had always longed for them to be friends, an idea that Dinah had rejected so vehemently that he never brought it up. Dinah looked down with disgust. The red gown that had been so lovely moments before was now covered in mud and a stray blond hair. She looked up at her father. He was staring at her. His blue eyes seemed to sear through her skin and bone, and she felt a seething hatred radiating out from the platform.

"Let us continue with the executions!" he declared. "You will have to excuse my daughter. She is a delicate and gentle flower, with a mind for those in need. Women by nature have weak and sensitive hearts, but your king shall never look away from justice!"

The feral cheering of the crowd swept over Dinah, and she numbly watched in silence as her father ordered the sword brought down again and again on the remaining prisoners, until there was only a bloody block left, and a clear sky above to witness it. She longed to close her eyes, but she kept them open, staring blankly at the proceedings, at the headless forms.

Later, she would return to the castle for the feast and ball that accompanied Execution Day. She would eat roasted birds decked with every imaginable spice, she would dance with Wonderland's most eligible bachelors as her father looked on, and she would try to smile and be gracious as members of the court worked to gain her favor with flattery. She talked of her upcoming coronation, of the king's justice, of what the ladies of the court were wearing this month, of her brother's latest hats. The conversations were hollow, dull, and easy to fake—she had learned long ago how to talk to an entire room without thinking once. But her mind never left the chopping block, her conscience whispering that she had caused an innocent woman to lose her head.

That evening, when the festivities were done and all was dark and still, Dinah excused Harris and Emily, and buried herself under the warm covers. The violent sobbing that followed left her physically exhausted and numb, and she fell asleep quickly. And so it would follow for the next few weeks—Dinah floated in a blank fog of disturbing thoughts or mindless tasks. She was fitted for her queenly gowns, instructed in the procedures and traditions of the coronation, and cooed over by various ladies and Cards. The royal jewels were sent over for her to choose from, and she let Emily do it. The sun rose and set, the days disappearing into the changing night sky, and yet Dinah couldn't be roused from her daze.

The coronation loomed just beyond her reach, something she had dreamed of her entire life, but Dinah found herself growing more distant from everyone and everything. Dinah marveled at the fact that what should have been the most exciting time of her life caused her to feel nothing but a gnawing fear and unease. Even as she tried on her coronation dress—a white-and-red monstrosity, and Harris chattered

with joy behind her, Dinah looked in the mirror and saw
Faina staring back at her. Her books were packed up and sent
to the royal library, her rooms made ready to house a queen.

Every minute of the day held rounds of eating and
dancing and croquet games, but Dinah was never content
until she sank deep into her covers at night, into a dreamless
sleep in which she saw neither blood nor Towers. Waking,
sleeping, none of it mattered. In a week, she would be the
queen, but all Dinah could feel was the heavy stone of guilt,
pressing hard against her chest, heavier with each passing
day. She gratefully surrendered to sleep, night after night, as
the stars whirled above.

$\mathcal{T}hirteen$

Dinah felt a feather on her hair.

No. Not a feather. A touch? An insect? A hand?

Dinah lurched up in her bed with a start, breathing heavily. She looked around her dark room. There was nothing—nothing but her curtains blowing in a cool breeze. She closed her eyes, willing the fear away.

Go back to sleep, she told herself.

Her spine tingled with dread. She opened her eyes again. Again, there was nothing—nothing but a faceless figure in a black hooded cloak standing beside her bed.

Dinah let out a terrified scream as a hand clamped violently over her mouth, black gloves cool against her lips. Her heart hammered wildly inside her chest, and she could feel all her limbs surge with strength. Dinah struggled ferociously, her hands reaching back, her nails clawing for the stranger's face, legs flailing beneath her. Finally, she threw her body forward, dragging the person onto her own back as she lay facedown on the bed.

They struggled as the stranger used most of his strength to keep his hand over Dinah's mouth. She screamed against the open palm, her inhale sucking the black leather halfway into her mouth. The stranger's mouth made it to her temple and a low whisper filled her ear.

"Shush now. Do not scream. Do not make a sound. Trust that I am not here to hurt you, Princess. You must trust me, you must. There is no time to explain. I could have slit your throat open five times by now, and yet I haven't. Nor have I stabbed you in your sleep. I am not here to harm you. Now, will you be silent?"

Dinah nodded and stopped struggling until the stranger gently lifted his hand from her mouth. Dinah bit her lip and thrust her elbow back into his face, feeling hard bone meeting flesh. The man gave a muffled roar as Dinah flung herself over the edge of her raised platform bed. She hit the ground hard, knocking the wind from her lungs. Willing herself to breathe, she frantically flailed her hands under the bed for something she knew was there, something that had been put there long ago, until finally her hands fell on a rusty hilt.

With a hard yank, Dinah emerged from under the bed with one of Wardley's old practice swords pointed at her aggressor. Her heart was beating so fast that Dinah feared it might explode. Her mouth opened and shut as she attempted to speak. Words came out quickly, interspersed with gulps of air. "Who—who are you? Do not come any closer or I will kill you. Tell me now, I demand it!"

The stranger in black shook his head. The voice was muffled under the black cloth—he was obviously taking pains to disguise his cadence as well. Dinah did not recognize the voice that spoke.

"I cannot tell you that, not tonight. There will come a time when you will have every answer you seek, I promise.

But now I need you to listen to me, listen to me as you never have before. It was I who sent you to Faina Baker."

Dinah held the sword unwavering, pointed at the stranger's chest. Black stars had started to form in her vision. She needed to breathe. The figure moved in a menacing circle around the bed.

"Don't come any closer," Dinah snapped. "Do not touch me again."

"I will not, Your Highness. I have no desire to hurt you. You do not have much time."

The figure paused, long enough that Dinah felt her hand tremble around the hilt.

"Forgive me for my bluntness. I wish there was another way to tell you, but it must be done. Your brother is dead. The king is planning to tell the kingdom that you killed him, killed him because you feared that he would take the crown that you have so obviously desired."

Dinah lost all feeling in her body. She had no mind to process her thoughts, no body to control. She was numb. Only her tongue worked. "You're lying. You're *lying*!" Her scream echoed through the empty chamber. The figure remained silent and still.

"I'm sorry, Your Majesty, but it is a devastating truth. It truly grieves me to tell you in such a manner. Your brother is dead, but you may live. Allow me to rephrase: do as I say and you *might* live. I have brought you a bag full of everything you may need. Take it and leave the castle. Leave this very minute."

Dinah now noticed the wide burlap bag at the stranger's feet. She could not process what was happening.

"Charles is dead? By whose hand?"

The stranger ignored her questions. "Do not tell anyone where you are going. To protect your servants, they must remain ignorant. I have rendered them both unconscious. They sleep soundly and safely in the other room." The stranger shuffled toward Dinah. He was growing agitated. "Princess, you stand in front of me when you should be moving. You can either leave or die, those are your choices. Your father won't wait for Execution Day to take your head."

Dinah looked up in disbelief. "My father? My father wouldn't kill me. I'm his . . . heir."

"Your ignorance is staggering, Princess. Your father

wishes to kill you. He will not share a crown with you, with anyone."

"Charles, my brother—"

"Is dead. By the king's hand," the voice replied flatly. "The Mad Hatter sings no more. You will no doubt grieve for him later, but now you must act. We are ahead of the king's plan tonight, but not by much, perhaps an hour. My queen, it's time to go."

Time seemed to stop as Dinah stood paralyzed in the darkness. The sword in her hand lowered slowly. She smelled the sweet scent of the Julla Tree blowing in through the open window and stared at Emily's shawl draped lazily over her dresser. The Wonderland moon blazed bright through the balcony windows, outlining the stranger as if he were made of stone.

"I can't . . . I don't . . . I'm supposed to be queen."

"And yet if you do not leave this night, you will die."

Something in the finality of his voice ripped her violently into the present. Dinah ran to the closet, grabbing her heaviest gray wool cloak and her mother's favorite slippers. The gray cloak buttoned easily over her long white sleeping gown. She pulled the hood over her tangled hair and grabbed the bag from the floor. Everything was fractured as she pulled herself together—she couldn't think straight. She tied Wardley's rusty sword so that it crossed over her shoulder. The stranger stood frozen in front of the window.

"Time is ticking, Princess. *Tick-tock*. You must go."

She grabbed the doorframe to keep her balance, realizing that this would be the last time she would ever see this room. Her voice quivered as tears welled in her eyes. Her brother. Dead? It couldn't be so. "How do I know that I can trust you? Why should I believe anything you say?"

The figure turned to the balcony. "If you wait much longer, you won't need to ask. There are many people in this castle with dangerous agendas. Mine was to see you crowned. But today it is to see you live. I pray that we will see each other again." The figure spun around and pointed to the door. "Now run. Go straight out of the palace. Do not stop for anything or anyone. If someone tries to stop you, *kill him*."

Dinah plunged out the door, tears running freely down her face. The wide stone hallways were pitch-black in the night hours, lit only by a few torches and the moonlight streaming through the stained-glass windows. Dinah sprinted through alcoves and stairways, doing her best to stifle the heavy sobs violently ripping her chest apart. She could tell almost instantly that something was amiss, for the palace was oddly still. Normally Heart Cards were stationed outside each of the castle apartments and stairwells, but now there were only open doors . . . and no Cards to be seen anywhere.

As she tore through the shadowy hallways, it occurred to Dinah that the stranger had been telling the truth about *something*. The walls themselves rippled with tension; there was a discomfort in the air. Wonderland Palace itself seemed to seethe with unrest. Dinah sprinted through the dark, vaguely aware in which direction she headed. She could only see her brother's face, his blue and green eyes peering up at her with pure adoration. *Charles. Charles.*

Her lungs burned with the effort of running as the bag bounced off her hip, the sword tight across her shoulders. She turned a corner and skidded to a stop as two drunken Spades strolled down an intersecting hallway before her.

There was nowhere to hide. She was in the middle of a wide corridor. Dinah froze, certain that the guards could hear her heart pounding in her chest, her loud breathing, the sound of tears dripping off her face.

An eternity passed as they strolled past her, their eyes focused straight ahead, the sound of their laughter bouncing off the walls. From there on, Dinah clung to the walls, staying in the shadows as she wove her way through the palace, her face rubbing up against thick cobwebs and scurrying spiders. Charles's apartment was in the westernmost end of the castle, and Dinah was out of breath by the time she reached the hallway that led to his atrium. Trembling, Dinah set the bag down and ducked behind a massive statue of Stern Ravier, the greatest Club Card who had ever lived, killed in a battle with the Yurkei.

She peeked around his leg muscles. There were two Heart Cards standing in front of Charles's open door. Wind whistled down the corridor, the door bucking in the breeze. She leaned back against the statue, her heart fluttering with panic. *What would Wardley do? He would send them away somehow*, she thought. *But if I try to do that, it will be my blood left behind.* Dinah untied the bag. Inside were a few pieces of clothing, loaves of bread, and a seemingly random collection of items. She shook her head. There was a strange metal contraption at the bottom. It looked like some sort of ratchet with wheels, moving parts, and a siphon. It would do. Dinah closed her eyes, said a silent prayer, and flung it down the adjacent hallway with all her might. It landed with a loud metal clatter that ricocheted up and down the palace walls. The Heart Cards, well trained, didn't hesitate. Swords drawn, they ran in the direction of the sound.

Dinah pulled her cloak around her and slipped silently through the door into Charles's apartment. All was still. The room was a bizarre tomb—a monument of hats, stairways, and twisted furniture. The animals painted on the domed ceiling watched Dinah, their mouths forever open in macabre smiles. Clear white moonlight fell in through open windows, illuminating a shiny red ribbon in front of Dinah's feet. Horror spread through her veins as her eyes followed the ribbon into an open closet near the front of the room. Walking slowly, she made her way over ankle-deep hats to the door. It inched open slowly, and Dinah prayed that she wouldn't see Charles's face. Instead, she saw the lifeless open eyes of Lucy, staring straight at Dinah, her throat a river of black blood. Quintrell was slumped over her, his dagger lying beside him on the floor. His taut muscles looked like stone in the dark light, ruined only by the rivulets of blood that ran down them. His throat also had been opened, his chest stabbed. Dinah clamped both hands over her mouth as she opened her throat in a silent scream, and rocked back and forth, struggling to hide her loud sobs. Then she reached out and shut their eyes with her fingers.

She heard the stranger's voice in her head, again and again. *Time is ticking, Princess.* Tick-tock. *You must go.* She raised her head. "Charles?" she whispered, daring to hope. "Charles?"

Only the darkness answered back, howling wind from an open window. *The window* . . . her gaze drifted up to Charles's favorite staircase, where an open window creaked and slammed in the violent wind. *Oh please*, thought Dinah, *oh gods, no.* She rushed up the winding staircase, for once not aware of how dangerous it was, a staircase that seemingly led to the heavens, a staircase with no railings and cluttered with hats of every color and shape. She followed the corkscrew up and up, climbing without thinking, her feet slipping precariously on the edges of the thinning wood.

As she reached the top, she paused to breathe, clutching her abdomen. Stepping carefully, Dinah leaned over the window ledge, praying that she would see nothing, anticipating the cool air on her face and nothing more. There were no stars out tonight—they had migrated north. Perhaps they rested on the surface of the Todren, light on that distant water. It took all her willpower to cast her eyes down, and when she did, a whimper escaped her lips. Under the window, maybe a hundred feet down, was a stone precipice that jutted out from the palace kitchens. The wide stone slab, perfectly square, lay below, Charles's tiny body splayed awkwardly across it. His back was bent at an unnatural angle, his head tilted toward the starless night sky, his features slowly becoming illuminated in the coming dawn. His eyes were open, blue and green, forever looking and never seeing. His mouth curved up in a half smile at Dinah, and his pale face was unblemished by the dark spot that blossomed from the back of his head.

Hats lay all around him. They had obviously fallen out with him. Scattered along the stone slab were some of his greatest creations—a sapphire top hat, a mossy green pillbox with lion-hair stitching, hats made of pink woven silk and peacock feathers. These pieces were proper funeral decor for the Mad Hatter, for a life so violently lost. Violently taken. A bird fluttered above his head in the dark, landing near his shoulder. Charles didn't move as the bird poked curiously at his flesh. Dinah turned and vomited on the staircase, her stomach emptying between wrenching sobs. She collapsed onto the edge of a coatrack that perched vertically out from the wall. Everything stopped.

I could stay here, she thought, closing her eyes. *I could just stay here and wait for them to kill me. I'll join Charles and Mother, Lucy and Quintrell, and we will all be together.*

Her heart clutched with raw grief, but something else, something hungry, was clawing its way up her stomach, spreading its poison, its delicious red fury rushing through her limbs. It alarmed and seduced her, this fierce anger. Dinah forced herself to stand. She looked down once more upon her brother's face, her eyes lingering on the way his dirty blond hair flopped over his forehead, the way his fingers curled, the color of his green eye. Making the sign of the heart over her breastbone, she whispered quick prayers over his broken body, praying that the gods would welcome him to their heavenly realm with love and kindness.

"It's time for me to go," Dinah whispered to his still body. A choking sob rose up in her throat as she realized this would be the last time she ever saw his face.

"I love you. I'm so sorry."

Dinah felt as though she were ripping apart as she turned down the stairs, so reluctant to leave him. Sobbing, she made her way down the stairs and slipped silently toward the back of Charles's chamber, pushing back the towering racks of millinery supplies. The door to the button room had been pulled open as well, a lock dangling loosely from its hinge.

Another sob wrenched its way out of her. The crown was gone, the table empty. His gift to her taken. Now there was not even a small piece of Charles left for her, only his shattered body on a stone slab. Anger rose up inside her as she stood before the empty table. It was all gone. She stayed a few seconds longer in the darkness, willing her body to be strong, willing herself to be brave. Pulling the hood of her cloak over her head, she walked silently back to the door. She inched it open without making a sound. The two Heart Cards stood silhouetted in the moonlight, their backs to Dinah.

"Do you reckon she really did it?" one of them asked, turning the metal siphon over in his palm.

"I'm not sure," the other one said, and laughed. "She would have to be a monster to kill her own brother, eh? Perhaps the pressure of the coronation was too much. What do you reckon will happen when the king wakes her up, sword to her throat?"

The first Card shrugged. "She'll be beheaded, either that or put into the Black Towers, no doubt. So long as I get food in my belly and a warm bed at the end of the day, I don't give a horse's ass if the princess or the duchess or the Mad Hatter sits on the throne."

"The Mad Hatter won't be doing that now, that's for sure. Pity, I never could afford one of his hats."

The other Heart Card gave a chuckle. "What's stopping you now?"

Dinah's hands shook as she pulled the sword from behind her back. It slid from her hilt without a sound. She replayed Wardley's lessons during their swordplay: *Hold the sword tightly. It is a part of your body, an extension of your strength, not a tool you use. Swing with force. Let your emotions radiate through the blade instead of through your mind.*

The hungry fury she had felt on the staircase swam in front of her eyes as she stepped out of the darkness, close enough that for a second, the guards could feel her breath on their necks. The first one went down easily enough with a thrust through the back of his neck. Dinah felt her sword meet tissue and bone, felt it slide through his flesh. His blood flecked Dinah's face. It was warm and mingled with her tears.

Pulling her sword back out was harder than she anticipated and required both hands. She gave a hard yank and his body fell forward, dead before he hit the ground. The second Card stared at her in shock. Dinah brought the pommel of her sword across his temple as she had seen Wardley do. He dropped to his knees, and she ran the blade swiftly through his chest. A stain of red bloomed out, becoming one with the crimson heart of his tunic.

I'm sorry, she thought, as she stood behind the bodies. *I'm sorry for this*. Dinah retrieved her bag from underneath the statue and gave a lingering glance back to the empty doorway of Charles's apartment. The glass doors rocked slightly back and forth in the wind, never giving a peek at the nightmare within. *Good-bye, Charles*, she thought. *Good-bye, my dear one*. She glanced down at the bodies in shock. Then she ran. She ran faster than she ever had in her life, plunging through the palace hallways one after another, taking turns without thinking. Her legs burned and her lungs contracted, but she never wavered—she had to get outside the palace. Dawn was beginning to break, and a pale morning mist had begun to filter through the carved-iron windows. Flinging open a side door, she approached the servants' quarters through the kitchen, where she dashed past several cooks making breakfast. They stared at her with wild confusion as she rushed past them, knocking over plates and trays.

"Your Highness?" several cooks called out to her, but she couldn't stop. The kitchens eventually led out to the courtyard, and she flung open the doors with a sigh of relief and stepped outside. The change in the light was so extreme that Dinah stood still for a minute, willing her eyes to adjust. She was in the trellised gardens that bordered the courtyard. White roses she had planted a lifetime ago with her mother were beginning to show, their early spring buds poking forth from their ivy blankets. Dinah straightened her bag and ran through the yard, keeping close to the walls, thankful that the trellis offered shelter from curious eyes.

At the sound of raised voices, she stopped and ducked behind a bush, elaborately trimmed in the shape of a dodo. Her whole body shaking, she tentatively raised her head over the prickly leaves and clenched her teeth. There he was—her father, marching through the courtyard with Cheshire at his side, leading what looked like an entire army of Heart Cards into the castle. His face was blotchy and red, full of a righteously blazing wrath.

"Halt!" All the Cards stopped moving, and Dinah felt her pulse quicken. Had he seen her? The King of Hearts's booming voice echoed over the marble pavement as he turned to address them. His hands shook as he screamed at the Cards. "Heed my orders and find my daughter! Should she try to run or fight, use any force necessary to subdue her. If this means at the cost of her life, so be it! She is guilty of murdering my innocent son, of high treason, and of planning the eventual demise of Wonderland. She is no longer a princess; she is a murderous traitor to the realm! We will wake her from her slumber and bring her to justice this very day. I will have her head by nightfall!" Cheshire grinned nastily, his hand wrapped around one of the Diamond's telltale dagger handles. The king turned and drew his Heartsword. "To the Royal Apartments!"

The Heart Cards marched two by two into the castle. Dinah began to shake uncontrollably. It was true, it was all true. Her father was a murderer. He killed her brother, killed Lucy and Quintrell. *You killed two guards*, a quiet voice reminded her. *You are not so innocent yourself.* Dinah wiped the sweat off her face. The truth of her situation dawned on her. There would be no talking through this, no plea from daughter to father. No compromise. It was over. She would not wear a crown, and she would not wear her head if she stayed here. The stranger had been right—she needed to leave the palace now, and never return.

Run, she whispered to herself, though her lungs tight-ened at the idea. It was not long before her advantage would disappear into the bright morning buzz. She followed the courtyard walls, making her way to the stables. The trellis ended, and Dinah waited until she could see no one lurking through the glaring morning light before sprinting toward the outside stalls. Keeping her head low, Dinah entered the stable labyrinth and began to weave her way through, one rivet and stall at a time. Around and around and around she went, circling deeper into the dark wood. The horses snorted and bucked as she passed them, their gentle senses picking up her panic and disorientation. *Almost there*, she thought, as she passed one stall after another, her feet slipping in mud and manure. The paddock she was looking for appeared, and for the first time that night, Dinah dared to hope she might make it out of this day alive.

Fumbling, she unhooked the latch and stepped into Speckle's stall. Someone was waiting for her. A man stood in front of her, the darkness of the stables concealing his features, his sword drawn. Dinah pulled back her hood and rested her hand on her sword. "Who is there?"

"Dinah?" whispered a voice.

"Wardley?"

They rushed together, falling gratefully into each other's arms. Dinah clutched him with desperation. Wardley kissed her forehead, her head, placed his hands on her cheeks.

"Are you hurt? What is happening? Dinah, what's happened?"

Dinah let the sobs she had been holding in since she saw Charles's broken body escape from her trembling lips. "Charles. Wardley, Charles is dead! Someone pushed him from his window. Oh gods." She buried her face in Wardley's Heart tunic. "I saw him, his little face, his neck, his head. And Lucy and Quintrell, their throats were slit—by a Heartsword, I'm sure of it. And I, I killed two Cards trying to escape."

Wardley pushed her back and stared at her face in disbelief. "But who . . . what?"

"My father. An assassin? I don't know what's happening."

"But why, why would your father kill his own son? What kind of a father would kill his own *son*?" Wardley's eyes showed disbelief.

"I don't know! The kind of father who does not want to share the throne. He killed Charles so he could blame it on me. Wonderland would never accept a queen who commits fratricide. My father wants my crown, Wardley. I don't think he ever intended to give it to me."

She shook her head as Wardley forced her to drink water out of a canvas horse bag. It splashed down her face.

Her voice rose to hysterics. "I don't know, I don't understand what's happening. A stranger woke me and told me to leave, but I didn't listen, I went to Charles's apartment to see and . . ." Dinah felt the tack room spin around her. "I heard him—my father. I *saw him*. He ordered the Heart Cards to arrest me and kill me if necessary."

Wardley nodded. "I heard. I managed to slip out the back of the march. We were woken up by the king, ordered to be present for your arrest and trial this morning, ordered to either kill you or take you into custody."

Dinah took a step backward. "What are you saying?" She looked down at Wardley's drawn sword. "You aren't?"

Wardley gave Dinah an exasperated look. "You can't be serious, Dinah." He wrapped her swiftly in his lean arms and murmured into her black hair. "You are my best friend. My queen. You will not die today, not on my watch. But you must go. Once your father has discovered that you have gone, this will be the first place he looks. He will kill us both. Dinah, you must go now!"

Dinah nodded and reluctantly pulled back from Wardley. She saw tears glistening in his brown eyes. She pulled Speckle's saddle from the wall mount, her hands shaking.

"*No.*" Wardley grabbed her arm roughly, and suddenly she was being pulled through the labyrinth of stalls, deeper and deeper into the middle of the stable. His arm was firm. She could not squirm out of his grip.

"Wardley, what are you doing? Stop it! I have to leave!"

Wardley continued to pull her through the stalls. "You cannot take Speckle. Where will you go?"

"Speckle is my horse!"

"You will not be able to outride the Heart Cards on Speckle, not even if you had a day's lead. Speckle can barely handle an afternoon trot. He's old, Dinah!"

"Then give me Corning. You've always said he is the fastest horse in Wonderland."

"That he is," mumbled Wardley as they ran past stall after stall of rudely awakened horses. Their whinnies filled the air. "Even then, even with Corning, I'm not sure you could—"

He was interrupted by the blast of a hundred horns sounding out from the palace walls. The sound froze them both. Dinah's blood ran cold, and she found herself unable to move.

"They're coming for me," she whispered. "It's over."

Wardley's eyes narrowed. "You will not die today, Dinah. You will die with a crown on your head, subjects bowing at your feet." He pulled Dinah through the center of the labyrinth, running now. An iron stall door, twice the height of the other stall doors appeared before them. The chain that held it shut was thick as a man's arm—but Wardley had keys, since he had been the stable boy for so long.

Dinah felt her entire body tremble. "No, no! I can't. Absolutely not."

"You must." There was finality in Wardley's voice— the decision was made. "Hornhooves are much, much faster than regular horses. They can easily outrun a normal steed, and they can run for days without exhaustion."

"Yes, and they will kill a person because he is not their master, or because they are in a foul mood that day!"

Dinah was terrified of the Hornhooves. Wardley swung open the pen, revealing the three Hornhooves—two white and one massive black beast. Morte, her father's steed. *He came in the night, with the devil steed and many men.* The creatures backed into the corner of their pen, snorting angrily, pawing the ground until it began to crack and break under their massive weight. Morte towered over the other two Hornhooves, a colossal figure of glistening black muscle, more like a dragon than a horse. His hooves were larger than Dinah's head and covered with hundreds of bone spikes— perfect for impaling a head, knee, or torso.

Dinah's knowledge of Hornhooves ran through her head. They were not just faithful steeds—they were blood-thirsty creatures, warriors of their own choosing. They loved killing and hunting and death. In their battle frenzy, a strong Hornhoov could kill forty men. There was a painting of Morte in her father's study, rearing up before a Yurkei warrior, the heads of Yurkei tribesmen decorating his hooves as her father raised the Heartsword from astride his back.

"No," Dinah started looking around, bordering on hysteria. "There must be a place for me to hide—maybe in the hay, maybe in the rafters."

Wardley grabbed her roughly and lifted her off the ground, his arms wrapped around her waist. Morte had backed into a corner and was snorting angrily, boiling-hot steam hissing out of his giant nostrils, his black eyes wide with confusion. The steam could scald skin.

"Shh . . . shhh there . . ." Wardley approached Morte slowly, still holding on to Dinah, who was flailing in his arms. Morte tolerated Wardley, since he had fed him every morning for years as the stable squire. The animal's eyes focused warily on Dinah. She could hear commotion outside the stable now, the clanking of boots and armor, the yelling of townspeople.

"Damn it, Dinah, go now. Step up. Now, now!"

Her hands trembled as Wardley hoisted her up to his chest, her hands on his shoulders. With a rough shove, he vaulted Dinah onto Morte's back with so much force that she almost ended up on the ground on the other side. Morte snorted and backed into the stall door. Dinah let out a cry. She was kneeling now on his back, an ocean of glistening black muscle and bone. He was so wide—twice the width of Speckle. Her legs couldn't fit around him.

"How do I . . . ?"

"Straddle his neck, not his back."

She edged forward and placed her legs on either side of Morte's neck as he tried to nip at her with his sharp white teeth. He bucked once, twice, and Dinah clung desperately to his mane to keep her balance.

"He's restless. Your father kept him locked up inside for years. He'll run for you."

Wardley threw her bag at her. Dinah wrapped the straps over her shoulders. The noise outside grew louder. Cards were flooding into the stable. They would be on them in minutes.

"Come with me!" she cried.

"I can't leave," answered Wardley, avoiding her eyes. "Not yet. Someone has to protect your people when you are gone. What about Harris? And Emily?"

Dinah felt a whisper of doubt. "I don't think I can do

this without you." Morte bucked again. Wardley reached up and put his hand on Dinah's shin. He was barely able to reach her because of Morte's towering height.

"I will find you. Head for the Twisted Wood. You should be able to hide there. I promise, Dinah, I'll find you—you have my word." Morte reared up and kicked his front legs, narrowly missing Wardley's face with a razor-sharp spike. Dinah looked down at Wardley. He did not seem afraid. He believed in her. It made her feel stronger, even if just for a second.

"Wardley, I—"

"Stab me."

"What?"

Wardley handed her his sword, inlaid with a ruby pommel. "Take this, leave me your rusty one. Now, stab my shoulder."

He patted the fleshy part of his upper arm. "Hurry up. Gods, Dinah, don't think about it! *Stab me!*"

With a cry, Dinah brought the point of her sword down into Wardley's arm, feeling his muscle separate and tear. Crimson rushed out of him, his blood, the boy she loved, splashing onto the ground, splashing onto her hand. Wardley let out an agonizing scream of pain.

"Arrggghh . . . Dinah, you didn't have to do it so well!" He staggered out of the pen and began throwing open one stall door after another with his other hand. Dinah heard voices from the outside ring of stalls. The Cards were making their way in. They were trapped. She would die here, Wardley as well. Here in this stinking pen, in the scents of manure and hay. Morte was almost dancing now, his hooves coming up and down, excited by Wardley's blood. Dinah looked over at Wardley, unlocking every stall door he could. She told herself to remember the curve of his brow, the color of his hair, the tilt of his spine . . . but she didn't have time.

A Heart Card burst through one of the stall doors. His eyes widened with fear when he saw Dinah on Morte.

"She's in here! The princess! She's on the king's—"

He didn't have time to finish. Wardley had pushed the rusty blade through his back. The man fell face-first into a drinking trough. Wardley glanced at Dinah, their eyes meeting.

"It's time."

Dinah opened her mouth to object. She heard men shouting orders outside the stalls. Morte began to pound the ground with his huge hooves.

"I can't, Wardley. Wardley . . ."

She paused, not knowing if she would ever have the chance to tell him.

"I love you."

"Go!" screamed Wardley.

He brought the flat of his sword down across Morte's hindquarters. It was enough. Morte reared up and bolted forward. Dinah didn't even have time to see what happened to Wardley because suddenly they were plunging through the stable. Morte rushed straight out through the labyrinth of stalls, bursting through door after door. His massive knees hit the doors first, and huge shards of wood shattered out from the pens as Morte trampled everything in his path—doors, troughs, wooden benches, other beasts. Dinah was inundated by a shower of splinters, but could do nothing more than cling desperately to his mane. His breath was so loud it hurt her ears as he burst through wall after wall, pen after pen. Chaos reigned. Wood exploded all around her as horses and men screamed. She could sense Morte's wild desperation to get out of the stable, his drive to be free.

Heart Cards flooded the stable now, a sea of red and white, and they watched with a fascinated horror as Morte shot past them in a violent shower of wood and hay. The final rung of the circle was a stone paddock. She pulled back on Morte's mane, but nothing happened. He charged forward, ever faster, excited by the challenge. Morte easily vaulted the wall, and Dinah almost lost her balance, slipping down his neck before she was wrenched upright by his momentum when he hit the ground.

They were outside now, and the bright dawn blinded her vision, which eventually focused on a terrible scene, something out of nightmares. Heart Cards were swarming around them everywhere, swinging their swords in her general direction as she flew past them. A brave Heart Card ran out in front of Morte, putting his hands up to stop him. Dinah motioned him out of the way, but he stood firm, his hands out in front of him.

"Whoa! Whoa!" Her screams were useless. Morte surged ahead, and his huge hooves trampled the man's head into pulp with a sickening crunch. Dinah's stomach turned, but she couldn't look away. She heard terrified screams from behind her and glanced back. The two other Hornhooves were running loose among the Heart Cards now, their hooves already soaked with blood. Dinah turned her head back around as Morte's body surged beneath her hips. The iron gates that sealed Wonderland Palace from the outside were growing closer with every second, and Morte showed no sign of slowing. People were shouting behind her, all around her, but one voice rose above the chaos—her father's booming tone.

"*Kill her! Kill her!*" She felt fear twist deep inside. Cards of every type were now trying to stop them. A Club Card flung a pot of burning oil toward them from a watchtower, but Morte was moving too fast and it barely splashed the end of his tail. They were flying through the market now, passing dozens of carts and tables covered in fruit and tarts.

A filthy little girl stood beside her mother, selling bread. She pointed at Dinah as they flew past, tugging on her mother's skirt. "Look, Mama, the princess!" she said, before falling to her knees.

Dinah's hood had fallen off long ago, and her loose black hair whipped around her face as she clung to Morte. Dinah felt her bag slipping from her shoulder. Praying that she would keep her balance, she reached around and wrapped the bag's cords over her back. Wardley's sword bounced across her shoulder blades. Morte gave a deep huff of satisfaction, a pleased rumble. The animal's nostrils and mouth heaved with steam, but Dinah got the distinct feeling that Morte was just beginning. His speed grew, his hooves barely brushing the ground. They were moving so fast Dinah could barely make out the faces of the people she passed.

When I die today, thought Dinah as they neared the tall iron gates, *at least I will know what it feels like to fly*. The ornate gates of Wonderland were left cracked open every day, for travelers and traders to come and go into the palace as they pleased. All around the gates now, Dinah could see Cards scrambling to shut the doors. To each side, large metal winches crawled with Spades struggling to turn the rusty levers that hadn't been turned in years. Someone gave a shout, and the towering gates began closing toward each other, creaking shut inch by inch. On the left side, a tall, gray-haired Spade squinted in the sun as she neared. Dinah recognized him instantly—it was the Spade she had slapped that day on her way to the palace. He watched her with a fascinated look on his face as other Spades clamored around him, screaming and pointing at one another, pointing at her. His movement was tiny, so small that no one else would ever know, but Dinah saw it. His hand paused on the winch, just for a second. It was enough.

Morte plunged through the narrow opening, his broad shoulders clipping both sides of the iron gate, which then burst backward. The steed let out a whinny of pain as the gates cleanly sliced into him, but his speed never wavered. He had seen the open sky and the field of white flowers before him—he tasted the freedom denied him most days in the dark stables. There was a shimmer of movement under Dinah's legs as Morte flexed his muscles, and then, just when she thought they couldn't go any faster, Morte's pace quickened, his stride lengthening. She leaned, and Morte instinctively turned east, never slowing. Faster and faster, his speed gained a growing rhythm as they soared away from the castle.

Dinah heard the gates being pried open behind her and turned her head in despair. A small army of horses emerged, led by a large man riding a white Hornhoov. The King of Hearts. His Heartsword was raised above his head, and he was screaming Morte's name over and over again with a crazed look upon his face. Dinah gave a shudder. She had never seen her father be more himself than in this terrible moment, and she knew she would never again question whether he had thrown her brother from the window. He was full of hatred and fury, intent on her death. There was no doubt.

She turned away, her heart hammering in her chest, and clung to the monster's neck. Morte gave a happy whinny, and Dinah understood that he had just realized they were being pursued. Shivers of pleasure rippled down his back, and his relentless gallop took on a joyous feel as they flew over bare fields and streams, past towns and villages, and over hills, flying until the palace was nothing more than a white-and-red dot behind them. Wardley had been right—Morte showed no signs of exhaustion; rather his speed seemed to increase. For every step her pursuers took, the Hornhoov took six. He would run them off their feet.

Dinah glanced back periodically, but it wasn't long before the Cards saw the hopelessness of this pursuit. They fell back one by one as their horses collapsed, exhausted by this endless sprint. Only her father pursued now, but he was never able to gain on them, even astride the other Horn-hoov. Morte was stronger and faster than the females, and angry at his confinement. His heavy hooves pounded the wildflower-carpeted ground, the short-grass plain, the rocky sand. On and on, Morte overtook the fields and hills lead-ing to the Twisted Wood. The distance between Dinah and her father grew until she finally saw him turn back, a tiny speck of white in the distance. A whoosh of air released from her lungs and suddenly she dared to hope that she might live until nightfall. Her legs and buttocks screamed with pain with each gallop, her body slamming fiercely against Morte's muscled back again and again.

Dinah pressed her head against the side of the Horn-hoov's neck, a new weariness overtaking her. She was sure if she fell, he would keep running. Not only did he not care for his rider, but he also didn't even seem to remember that he had a rider. The fall alone would surely shatter her bones. If she fell off, he would keep going. Either that or he would circle back around to kill her, his giant hooves grinding her head into pulp. And she would let him.

They were heading due east now, so she leaned left, hoping to turn him more north, into the deeper parts of the Twisted Wood. His body responded, and he churned the mud out from under his hooves as they veered in that direction. *Go to the Twisted Wood*, Wardley had said. *I'll find you.* The trees on the horizon grew taller, their limbs reaching for the sky. The sun loomed high in the afternoon sky. They had been running for hours, for days it seemed.

Morte flew up a ridge and Dinah sat up with surprise, shading her eyes. She had almost fallen asleep against his immense neck. "My gods."

Now she could see it—the Twisted Wood. It lay directly ahead of them, its outer ring of trees as tall as the castle towers. Their spindly branches clutched hungrily at the sky. The trees leaned and moaned together, their limbs shifting ever so slightly, even though there was no breeze. Dinah looked in wonder at the wood, though Morte showed no signs of stopping. She held on. What else could she do as they sped closer to the tree line? Though the trees were gigantic, the wood had been farther away than it looked, and Dinah's legs were cramped, her thighs bleeding by the time they made the edge of the trees. Her throat was parched—water seemed like an enticing dream.

The sun began to set in the east as they neared the border. It had been a day and half a night since Dinah had been shaken awake by the stranger. Morte was finally showing signs of exhaustion as violent spasms began to surge up and down his neck and a violet-tinted foam dripped from his lips. The trees, taller than anything Dinah had ever seen, taller than the Black Towers, lay directly ahead, their ghoulish arms blocking out most of the waning light. Something in the trees gave a shimmer, so Dinah didn't see Morte's hoof land in a small hole, plummeting him forward.

The air took them quickly, and both were thrown violently toward a muddy creek bank. Dinah's body flew up and over Morte's as his rolled like thunder beneath her. Dinah landed on her side, the bag cushioning her fall. She rolled with a thud against an overturned tree, her head slamming into the withered trunk. Something in her hand snapped like it was a thin tree branch, and a blinding pain shot up her arm.

She tried to raise her head, but it was no use. She couldn't think. She couldn't move. Dirty water flowed into her open mouth as she struggled to stay awake. Her final thoughts were of Charles's eyes, brilliant blue and a soft green, as he poked his tousled head out from behind a staircase.

"My Dinah."

He had touched her hand lightly.

She closed her eyes and surrendered to the black, a queen no longer.

Fourteen

Dinah dreamed of drowning. She was twisting and floating, only this time instead of the inky substance of glossy
mirrors, she was actually inhaling water. The sea itself was
flowing into her mouth and lungs. Wriggling fish nested on
her tongue, minnows picked at her teeth. An eel, checkered
white and black, slithered over her body, wrapping itself
around her torso, her chest. Seaweed clung to her ankles as
she struggled to move, and she felt a growing panic that she
would never reach the surface.

Out from the black water swam something shadowy,

something huge and terrifying. Dinah blinked her eyes, crusted over now with bits of coral and sand. A shimmering white fish glided toward her. Its scales rippled in the sunlight, blinding her with its beauty. It opened its mouth and Dinah saw row after row of razor-sharp teeth. The fish was wearing a hat. She opened her mouth to scream and all the water rushed in.

Dinah opened her eyes with a start. There was water in her mouth, real water. She sputtered and choked. To her relief, the water was from a small stream, barely a trickle over a ground covered with mud and dying plants. Dinah turned her head and spat, gagging on a piece of grass that was stuck to her cheek. Hands shaking, she pushed herself up, only to have a stabbing pain race through her fingers. She looked down. Two of her fingers were swollen and distorted, both twisted in unnatural directions. She couldn't bend them, and touching them lightly caused her to cry out in pain. Still sputtering, Dinah sat back down and stared down at her fingers. *Take a breath. You have to think.*

After staring for a few moments, she reached down and yanked two thick blades of grass up from the stream bed and

wound her injured fingers together. Dinah let out a scream
when she cinched the knot; it felt like needles being shoved
under her nails. Breathless, she lay down facing the stream
where she could see her filthy reflection. Frantically, she
wiped the crusted blood off her face, which was scratched
from temple to chin. The muddy waters of the creek still
tasted foul on her tongue. She spat again and rolled over
before letting out a shrill scream. Black hooves covered with
thick bone spikes dug in inches from her face. Bloodstains
spotted the spikes—some fresh and dripping, some old.
From this close, she could see that the bones were jagged,
cut like a carving knife. This made them even more deadly
than a smooth blade when pushed into the sides of a man's
head.

Dinah raised her head slowly, hoping to not spook him.
Morte loomed over her, so large his frame blocked out the
afternoon sun. All she could see were heaps of black muscle
and bone. *He will kill me*, she thought. *He wants to*. Steam
hissed from his nostrils as the steed rocked his head back and
forth over her. His hoof raised and stomped down, inches
from Dinah's frame, so easily crushable, this sack of tissue

and bone. Morte stomped his hoof again. The ground trembled. He lowered his huge head and sniffed Dinah. Steam washed over her face, so hot that she feared her skin would blister. She didn't move, her body as still as stone, her eyes closed. Finally, Morte seemed satisfied and pulled his long muzzle back, stomping again.

Dinah opened her eyes and gave a terrified glance over at his hoof. One of the bone spikes had broken and was now pushed upward, several inches deep into Morte's foot. It must have happened when he stepped in the hole, she thought, and when he struggled he pushed it into himself. Marrow dangled from the end of it and Dinah felt her stomach heave. The huge hoof came down again in front of her face, breaking the hard ground as if it were made of glass. Dinah took a deep breath and raised herself slowly to her knees, her hands up in front of her, showing surrender. Morte bucked, his feet landing hard all around her. She stayed still until he stopped moving and then reached out her shaking hands until they hovered above the bloody bone spikes. He huffed angrily.

I could lose my hands, she thought, *either my hands or my head*. Reaching out with the utmost of care, Dinah placed her shaking hands on Morte's leg, running them slowly down together until they reached the hoof, as she had seen Wardley do a hundred times with normal horses. *Wardley.* What had become of him? Her hands rested now just above the bone spikes. She left the hand with the broken fingers on Morte's massively muscled leg while she wrapped the other around the bone spike that was impaled into the bottom of his hoof. The jagged edges of the spike pressed into her skin as she pulled downward. Morte let out a terrifying scream of pain and pounded the ground with his other hooves. The bone hadn't moved at all, except now it was slick with blood from Dinah's lacerated hand.

Morte gnashed his teeth together, and Dinah could sense his fury and anxiety growing. She had mere seconds before he lost control and killed her—she could feel it. She wrapped her hand once again around the bone spike and yanked with all her might, the skin on her hand ripping and tearing as if she was grabbing the end of a sword. Dinah let out a bloodcurdling cry as the bone scraped deep into her skin, sliding on the wet blood. Her blood mixed with Morte's as it dripped, and her high-pitched scream was matched by his as he knocked her roughly aside with his head. Dinah curled into the ground, her head under her hands, one of them holding the bloody bone spike as Morte stomped around her in a circle, his hooves inches from her body.

"Please . . . ," murmured Dinah. "Please."

Morte stood still, his huge eyes watching her. His hoof would twitch and he would quickly raise it, but then bring it back down slowly with a thud. He shook his head angrily back and forth, a swaying motion that shook his entire body. Dinah cowered in horror—she could tell the beast was considering taking her life. She stayed still, and after a few minutes, he stomped away to inspect his wound. When Dinah raised her head, he was staring at her from a dozen yards away, his huge black eyes taking in every inch of her face—he was thinking, calculating. After what seemed like an eternity, he gave a loud huff and bent his head to drink from the meager stream. Dinah sat back and let relief wash over her as she clutched her injured hand. Morte would not kill her, not right now, anyway. She washed her hand in the creek, blood tinting the water red before it traveled down-stream with a cluster of variegated purple leaves. She ripped off the hem of her once-white nightgown—now brown, bloody, and covered with coarse black hair—and wrapped it around her hand. Pain from her broken fingers swept over her and she wearily climbed out of the creek bed, fearing she might faint. Stumbling, she came to rest against the overturned tree she had smacked her head on, keeping an ever-wary eye on Morte, who was now happily eating every bit of foliage in sight.

Food. Dinah was suddenly aware of a gnawing emptiness in her stomach, a hunger stronger than she had ever experienced. Legs trembling beneath her, she pushed herself to her feet and walked very slowly toward her bag. She untied the strings, letting it fall open before her, and her hands searched wildly for food. It wasn't long until she found husks of dried bird meat, small loaves of bread, some apples, and fresh berries. Dinah ripped into the bread, chewing quickly and swallowing large chunks. She was convinced that nothing had ever tasted as good as this plain bread, and she followed it with a handful of berries. There was a small waterskin inside the bag, which she filled with water from the creek. The liquid was brown and muddy, but it still flowed down her throat like sweet nectar, and Dinah drank until she felt that she might be sick.

Her stomach full but unsettled, Dinah finally felt her mind begin to clear as she stared in horrified awe at Morte, his mane tousled wildly in the wind. The truth played over her mind in waves. Her father had killed her brother. The stranger had warned her, packed this bag, and sent her on her way. If she had followed his instructions, there would have been no chase. She would have slipped away quietly into the night, heading in whatever direction best suited her. But she had to see Charles, had to see his broken body, had to see Lucy and Quintrell piled on top of each other like old dresses in the closet. She had to see Wardley. Wardley, her love. Wardley had saved her, and she had stabbed him in return. What would happen to him? How would he possibly find her again? Would her father spare his life because of his liking for the boy, or would he take his head because of his loyalty to Dinah? Hopefully the king would see the very real stab wound she had given him and be convinced, but he was generally untrusting. What would become of Harris and Emily? A tear rolled down her cheek as she thought of her kindly guardian waking up and finding her gone. Would he believe that she had done it? That she had knocked him unconscious and killed her own brother? Dinah shook her head. *Never.* Harris knew her true self, but hopefully he had the good sense to hide his loyalty from the king.

The Twisted Wood gave a loud groan behind her, followed by the creaking of the trees consciously shifting their wide branches. Every time Dinah blinked she could see her father, the rage on his face, the Heartsword raised above his head, the bloody look in his eyes. He would have killed her if he had caught her, and he would kill her now if he caught up with her. Dinah quickly got to her feet, her thighs aching and raw from clenching them around Morte's neck. The King of Hearts would be coming back, with horses and Cards and trackers. Several of the Spades were trained in tracking, and they would find her easily out here.

Dinah took a look around to fully understand her situation. They were on the edge of the Twisted Wood, only three hundred feet of field before the trees—giant colossal trees that looked angry and unwelcoming. The clearing was lovely, a hilly field that hid a small creek bed, its rocky ground covered in spotted purple wildflowers and yellow shrubs. As Morte munched on wild grasses, the scene was almost picturesque—a rural fantasy, something she would paint in her art lessons. The raw beauty of the moment mingled with Dinah's lingering terror, and she clutched at her chest. The king would return; in fact, he was probably already on his way. She had to think, had to move. She didn't have time to linger on what had happened—this was not the time to grieve. Dinah scurried over to the bag. The stranger had packed clothing, along with a few tools and food—two white linen tunics, brown wool pants, a belt, undergarments, one heavy black dress, and deep-red riding boots—the boots of Heart Cards, she noted. Looking around sheepishly, Dinah pulled the thin white nightgown off over her head and shivered in the cool spring air as the breeze caressed her bare body. She pulled on the brown pants and a white tunic, and shoved her feet into the red riding boots. They fit perfectly. Moving quickly, she rolled up the nightgown and her wool cloak and shoved them back into the bag, both hands stinging with the effort.

She gingerly unwrapped the linen from her palm. The

wound was ugly: a thick black and bloody slash that ran the length of her hand. She rewrapped the cut before splashing a palm full of creek water on her face. The sun was high in the sky, and the warmth on her skin made her sleepy. *I have to focus*, thought Dinah as the wind blew her hair around her face. *I have to be smart or they will find me all too easily. I can't think about things like sleep right now.*

She bit her lip. Her father was brave, a man of massive physical strength. He was not, however, terribly clever. No, he left that up to Cheshire. It wasn't her father she had to outmaneuver, it was Cheshire. What would he do? *He would expect me to go north*, she thought. The Twisted Wood was full of dangers and mysteries, but most important, it was the outlying land of the Yurkei tribes. The Twisted Wood would bring only death, but in the north there were scattered towns in which she could take refuge, hide out, change into someone else. He would expect her to find her mother's family, who lived on the northern tip of the Western Slope, in Ierladia.

Behind her, the Twisted Wood groaned again, the trees simultaneously turning their branches to the sky by some unspoken command. Past the Twisted Wood lay the top-less Yurkei Mountains. That was the least-safe place for the Princess of Hearts, for it was a place of wild Yurkei, bent on the destruction of Wonderlanders. It was the last place her father would expect her to go. Perhaps that's why Ward-ley had suggested it. She looked fearfully at the wood as it moved slightly, alarmed by the unsettling feeling that she was being watched by the trees. Few men had lived to tell the tales of the Twisted Wood, but even fewer men had gone up against her father and survived. The decision was made. Morte nickered softly in the wind, seemingly enjoying the breeze on his face.

Dinah took note of the ground. *We are all over this place*, she thought. Both she and Morte had spilled blood here, left footprints, pieces of themselves. Any tracker worth his snuff would surely see that they had rested here. Dinah kicked a petrified piece of wood in frustration. It splintered into tiny shards. *I have to lead them away from here.* She looked at the sky. By her best guess, her father would have half a day's ride back to the castle and then a full day's ride back to her spot. She had been unconscious for maybe three hours, judging by the sun's location when she woke. Dinah silently thanked her guardian for all those hours spent on sun-tracking lessons, something she had constantly bemoaned as useless. Making a false trail was a gamble, but one she must take. She had to escape, and to do that, she had to lead the trackers away from her trail. She had to act differently from the way they would expect her to. It might not work, but she had to try.

Dinah picked up her bag and began walking northwest. Her feet groaned with each step, and both hands throbbed with sharp pains. Dinah found herself dreaming of sleep, of lying down in the thick grasses, which looked now as comfy as her down-filled palace mattress. She let her thoughts wander wildly as she staggered along. Who was the stranger? There was something familiar about him, but yet she wasn't even sure it *was* a man. The way the stranger had wrapped a hand around her mouth, the way the whisper had washed over her, it was all so absolute. Powerful. The more she thought about what had happened, the more frustrated she became. The night was a blur of intense fear and wild emotion, and she found her memory of the whole thing very blurry and filled with gaping holes. Had there been anyone else in Charles's room with her? She hadn't even thought to look. Was his head wound from the fall, or was it by a sword? How had she gotten from his room to the courtyard? What had happened to Wardley when she galloped out of the stable? Why hadn't he come with her? Why had Morte not listened to her father?

Overwhelmed by the questions, Dinah stumbled over a rock, her knees hitting the ground with a hard thud. Her mind collapsed inward. Was she responsible for Charles's death? She let her tears fall unabashedly for her beautiful brother, for Lucy, for Quintrell. All innocents, all slain by her father's hand. It was her fault that they were dead, her fault that Charles had sailed out an open window in the dark, starless night. Had he been afraid? Did he scream? Dinah offered up a silent prayer that he hadn't understood what was happening, that his last moments were peaceful and unaware. Had Lucy and Quintrell been killed after him, or before? She choked on a sob. Did Charles see their murder and run up the stairs to escape? Oh gods. Dinah covered her mouth, afraid she would be ill. She couldn't stay here, kneeling in this field, but she couldn't will herself to move either. She was paralyzed by her grief, sobbing. After a while, a tiny pebble near her hand wobbled and then rattled over the dirt. Hooves. She heard them. The ground vibrated with the sound of horses and Dinah lowered her head.

The thudding of hooves slowed as they approached and then stopped. Reluctantly, Dinah looked up, expecting to see the shiny reflection of a Heartsword. Instead, Morte stood beside her, his great head lowered so that Dinah could look straight into his huge black eyes.

"You followed me," she whispered, reaching out her damaged hand to stroke his nose. Morte jerked back in alarm and brought a hoof down very close to her head. Dinah cowered. *Not yet*, she thought, *not yet*. Wiping her eyes, her body shaking with the effort, Dinah rose to her feet and continued walking. She glanced behind her in amazement as Morte followed her, even when she slightly changed directions. His massive presence still unnerved her—she was duly aware that he would find joy in killing her, but it was nice not to feel alone.

Plodding forward ever so slowly, they walked for a few more hours, Dinah swallowed by her thoughts, Morte enjoying the sun on his dark hide. After careful consideration, she tossed him an apple from her bag and he swallowed it whole, not even bothering to chew it. Reaching in her bag, Dinah found a piece of dried bird meat and gnawed it hungrily as she fantasized about a steaming raspberry tart and a warm cup of tea. Before she even tasted it, the bird meat was gone. *I have to quit eating like this*, she thought. *What will I do when the food in the bag runs out? It's only been a day.*

The view around her was changing, and Dinah wondered how far she had gone. The sun simmered low in the eastern sky, and dusk would be upon them in hours. Low plains covered with wildflowers still continued on as far as Dinah could see, the view interrupted every now and then by a white tree dripping with silvery moss that rustled even when there was no breeze. Dinah realized that it wasn't the landscape that had changed so dramatically since they left their little creek—it was the *color* of the landscape. The wildflowers that had been thousands of different colors when they started out had begun subtly changing their hue the farther she walked. Clusters of delicate pansies, daffodils, thick delphinium, stalks of tall liatris, roses, and tulips were all beginning to shift their rich colors into cooler shades. Red larkspur began taking on a bluer hue the deeper she went. Yellow daffodils bleached white then turned into a light blue, then lavender. The color change seemed to blossom out from the stamen itself—a swirl, just a hint of a different shade, triggered the metamorphosis.

Her feet caressed the flowers' changing hues, field after field. It was so incredible that Dinah momentarily forgot how exhausted she was. It was miles of the same breathtaking, flat landscape before a large knoll rose from the ground before her, carpeted in mountain-blue flowers. It reminded Dinah of every picture she'd ever seen of the sea, a wave cresting just as it reached its highest peak. Looking up, Dinah could see that the color changed again just slightly on its peaked curve. Somehow the top of the hill was a different color than the base.

She dropped her bag with a thud. Forgetting everything, she ran swiftly to the top of the hill. Her movement startled Morte, who gave an alarmed buck, his hooves pounding the ground with irritation. When she reached the top, Dinah let herself collapse into the bed of flowers, gazing out at the most magnificent sight she had ever beheld, its beauty sucking all the air from her lungs. It was blue. The deepest blue she had ever seen, deeper than the cornflower blue of Vittiore's eyes, richer than her sapphire jewels. The most beautiful gowns in the kingdom could never capture this blue, this multilayered azure, pure blue that stretched out as far as the eye could see. Every hill, from here to the north horizon, was covered in blue flowers, all one shade; one perfect, deep blue spread over a thousand different types of flowers. She watched in amazement as a wind rippled through the valley and the blue shimmered from end to end, rolling in wave after wave.

As Dinah's mouth fell open in awe, a particularly strong gust swept through the valley, and she watched in wonder as the color shifted into the palest powder blue, instantly overtaking one flower after another, as if the flowers were whispering to one another. It was so fast that she could never catch its origin, see the first flower to change. Breath after breath, the flowers shifted their colors: turquoise to lavender, lavender to midnight blue so dark it was almost black. Dinah had never seen anything so beautiful. This was the

Ninth Sea, a darkened area in the center of the Wonder-land map, a name Dinah had written a hundred times in lessons. On the map it appeared as a body of water, but that was wrong. There was no water, only an ocean of blowing flowers—an endless expanse of blue against the darkening sky. Dinah realized with a start that not only had she gone far enough; she had gone too far north. She had lost track of time in her wandering, and nightfall was near.

Wonderland's stars began to appear in the sky; on this night they would be hanging directly overhead, low in the sky, but centrally clustered. They seemed brighter out here than from her palace balcony. She squinted east, her breath catching again as the flowers changed to a startling, striped blue. Yes, she had gone too far; they were beginning to inch away from the end of the Twisted Wood. Past the Ninth Sea was a huge expanse of nothingness, which ended at the Todren, exactly the direction her father saw her riding last, and the direction she wanted him to follow. It was time to walk back. She gave one long, lingering look at the Ninth Sea rippling in the wind, the colors shifting from breeze to breeze, never the same blue twice. *I could stay here all day*, she thought, *just fade into the blue, disappear.*

She picked a flower near her feet to toss back into the sea, but it withered and died in her hand. Dinah released the dust instead, and it danced in the wind over the shifting waves of lapis. *I wish Charles could see this.* The thought made her chest ache. She let out an exhausted sigh and turned around. Morte looked confused as Dinah carefully backtracked, but soon he followed suit, placing his hooves into the prints they had made just a few hours ago. Dinah was stumbling frequently now, her exhaustion made dreadful by the overwhelming ache in her right hand and the stabbing pain of her left hand. She was so tired. *I won't make it,* she thought, *I won't make it back.* Her heart felt like it was pounding outside her chest, its beat thrumming in her ears. She stumbled over her feet again and again. Every other step ended on her knees. Finally, Dinah stayed down, closing her eyes to the bright stars above. *I'll just rest,* she thought. *Just for a moment.* Morte stood impatiently over her until he finally nudged her roughly with his huge nose, the steam from his nostrils singeing the hairs on her arm. With a punishing effort, Dinah pushed herself up, her legs obeying when her mind could not. Morte lifted his hoof and brought it down hard on the ground, repeating the gesture.

"What do you want?" she pleaded angrily. "Let me sleep!"

Morte stared at her blankly until it occurred to her: he wanted her to ride him. The thought made her glad, but she was unsure how to get onto him. She sometimes had a hard time mounting Speckle, and Morte was twice his height and had no saddle. Using his mane to get up seemed a sure way to die a painful death, plus she could never muster the energy to pull herself up. Morte lifted his hoof again and held it aloft, then brought it down with a resounding thud.

Oh. Her body trembling with exhaustion, Dinah laid her hand against Morte's side. She could feel the monstrous heaving of his ribs, the pounding of his strong heart. He lifted his hoof. She gently placed her boot on the end of the spikes, balancing ever so carefully, aware that the spikes could easily impale her foot if the weight wasn't distributed right. Eyes closed, she mumbled a tiny prayer and stepped up. The spikes pushed deep into her boot as Morte lifted his leg. Dinah flew up, up, up until she was at the right height to pull herself onto Morte's back. His expansive back was comfortingly warm. The muscles of her legs gave a painful throb as they resumed their position straddling Morte's thick neck, but she could not have been more grateful to be sitting. They both sat still for a moment. Dinah raised her voice to command him and then thought better of it. She sat quietly until Morte broke into a trot back in the direction they came, putting his hooves directly into the prints that he had made earlier. It was not the mad sprinting that had brought them here, but it was three times faster than Dinah would have gone if she had been able to sprint the entire way. The motion cradled her, and Dinah closed her eyes, resting her body against his large head. She fell asleep quickly.

The striped Wonderland moon was high in the sky when the ceasing of Morte's trotting woke her. She looked around and let out a happy sigh when she recognized the field, the creek bed where they had originally begun. How quickly this had come to seem like a safe place, this tiny valley. She slid down Morte's side, unsure of how else she would get down from his towering height. Her leg brushed one of the bone spikes, which left a thin scrape down the length of her shin. Morte took deep gulps from the creek, and Dinah filled her waterskin for the second time. It was time to move; her father was probably closing in on them. She had walked too far, but hopefully it was enough—enough to throw off the trackers, enough to fool Cheshire. She said a silent prayer that they would take the bait.

Dinah began limping toward the woods, relieved to hear Morte's heavy footsteps following her. Several of the colossal trees guarding the edge of the wood twisted their trunks slightly in her direction as she walked past. Dinah let her hands play across her sword hilt, reassured by its presence. *I will not be afraid of this wood*, she told herself, *because my fight to live does not begin now. I have been fighting all my life, I just didn't know it. My fight began when I was born to my father, who feared the day I would assume the throne, and I am safer in these woods than I ever was in his palace. I did not die today, so I will not fear death tomorrow.* The thought gave her courage, though she doubted that her courage would remain. She looked back at Morte, following several hundred yards behind, his ears pressed flat against his head. Even the deadly Hornhooves feared the Twisted Wood. Fear churned the insides of her stomach. Dinah drew her sword, and with that, the former Princess of Wonderland and her black devil steed disappeared into the Twisted Wood, leaving nothing behind but a false trail and the distant whiff of a crown.

♥

Back at the palace, the king paced the floor angrily as six Heart Cards struggled to dress him in his armor.

"Hurry up! We're losing time. Cheshire!"

His adviser seemed to curl directly out of his innermost thoughts.

"Yes, my lord?"

"Are the Cards assembled?"

"Of course."

"And they are our best Heart Cards, are they not?"

"Yes, they are all ready. We will find her, my king. Have no doubt. She is bound to be exhausted and desperate after her night of murder. That is, if the Hornhoov didn't kill her already."

"One could only hope. Argh! That foul little creature. I will throw her in the Towers and forget that she was ever called mine."

Cheshire bowed down in the long shadow of the throne, kneeling timidly before the king, his purple robe flowing down the steps.

"If Your Majesty trusts me, I think I have found a way to trap her. I have heard of a man, a great tracker, a Spade. I believe he can find her for us."

The king stood.

"Bring him to me."

A wide, predatory smile crept across his adviser's face, distorting his jaw, his teeth gleaming white.

"How fine you look when dressed in rage."

READ ON FOR AN EXCERPT FROM

BLOOD OF WONDERLAND

The Cards had found her. The sounds of faint shouts and clinking armor seemed to be coming over a dark ridge in the distance.

Tears welled up in her eyes and her hands shook as she clutched Morte's mane, turning him around, racing away. As he ran, the sun sank into the cloudy horizon and all was black. The Twisted Wood became nothing more than shadows, an inky blur of trees and branches. Dinah could barely see Morte's head in front of her as he dived through the trees, straining to outpace the growing sounds of horses and men. The cacophony was coming from all sides now, so foreign and abrasive to her ears after so much silence. Morte's arrival desecrated the quiet wood, violating the peace of the trees, the hum of the insects. She couldn't see where her pursuers were, but they were getting closer—and there was nowhere to run where they wouldn't hear Morte crashing through the brush.

Dinah drew her sword and the ring of metal echoed through the trees. She wouldn't be able to fight through many of them—any of them, maybe—but she would not be taken to the Black Towers. She would force them to kill her, and she would try her best to kill her father. That was her only purpose on this night; if this was going to be the way it ended, so be it. She would avenge her brother, his keepers, and lastly her mother, killed by her father's neglect and cruelty. Dinah sat still and held her breath for a moment. Then her father's voice carried through the darkness, commanding his troops, the sound sending a dagger of fear straight through her.

"She's here! Bring her to me, dead or alive. A lifetime's worth of wages and a position in the court will be given to the Card who finds her. Do your duty and avenge your innocent prince! His blood will not be in vain!"

The voice stopped Dinah cold—Morte as well. They

stood perfectly still as the roar of soldiers echoed all around them in the darkness. They were surrounded. A leaf crackled directly behind Dinah, and she heard deep breathing.

"Hide," whispered a voice in the darkness. "If you want to live, don't fight. Hide."

Dinah didn't need to be told twice—or have time to consider the source of her advice. She quietly dismounted Morte and bid him to follow her into a densely leafed area of the trees, stumbling many times over things she could not see. Something slithered over her boot and she forced herself not to scream. It was a consuming darkness. *The stars must be on the other side of the sky tonight*, she thought, *hiding from this terrible noise.* The sounds of the Cards were all around her—the violent breaking of tree branches, the clanking of cups against thighs, horses pawing the ground, and a singular sound that chilled her blood—the thundering sound of another Hornhoov crashing through the brush.

She stood still, considering how to best hide—and to hide Morte. She looked over at him in the darkness but could see almost nothing—the black of his coat blended effortlessly with the trees and night. *I have to disappear*, she thought. *Disappear into the night. The dress.* Moving as quickly as she dared, Dinah untied the flaps on her bag and rummaged through it, her hands feeling for the thick, heavy fabric. When it seemed she had touched everything in her bag except for what she needed, Dinah's hand felt it. She pulled out the dress, unfurling it against the starless night. Dinah could barely see her hand in front of her face, let alone the pitch-black fabric of the dress. Dropping her sword to the ground, she pulled the dress over her head. It slipped over her easily, the ends of the dress brushing the ground. Reaching back, she felt that the dress collar was lined with a hood. Dinah pulled the black wool over her dark hair and face. It was long enough to cover everything, and the fabric dusted her chin. She pulled her hands into the sleeves so that they would not show and inched up next to a particularly wide tree, leaning into the trunk.

The voices were almost on top of her now—they would be on her in seconds with their swords and horses and torches. She looked over at Morte, who stood as still as she did, white steam hissing out of his nostrils. It was taking every inch of his control not to leap into the fight. Dinah reached out and felt for his nostrils. She gently and carefully laid her hand over his muzzle. Her voice shaking, she murmured, "Still . . . still. . . ." The steam stopped and Morte knelt on the ground, becoming one with the thick foliage around him. Perhaps the animal knew he could not win this fight, not tonight, not while he was still partially wounded from the bear. Either way, Dinah could no longer see him. She pressed her face and body up against the tree and waited for them to come. Quivers of fear crawled up from her legs and infested her chest. Her knees felt weak. She clutched at her heart.

"Don't move," whispered the same voice from before. Was it above her? "Don't move, don't breathe, and the Cards shouldn't see you." Dinah froze, a black statue in the woods. She closed her eyes as the Cards swarmed around them. Several Cards trampled right past her—it sounded like one almost tripped over Morte before he suddenly changed direction and veered to the right. *He should be thankful to be alive*, she thought, *as that would have ended in his very gruesome death.* Two brushed past the tree she was leaning against, and Dinah clenched her hands inside the sleeves to keep from fainting.

Unable to raise her head for fear of being seen, Dinah kept her eyes glued to the ground. She could see nothing except the occasional flash of a torch as it was waved in the darkness, the woods swallowing the light in their vast space.

The voices of the Cards flowed past the trees. "She was here!" "I heard her, Your Majesty!" "She's over there!" The cacophony of sounds bouncing through the woods made it very hard to tell where each man was—and she could see that the Cards were disoriented and scattered. They were unaccustomed to the trees, to the starless night. To Dinah's horror, she felt the earth shake beneath her feet and heard the singular plodding with which she had grown so famil- iar. She dared to raise her face a few inches. The white Hornhoov carrying her father had entered the trees, with Cheshire's sleek stallion following behind him. Her father sat proud and furious atop a female half the height of Morte but still gigantic. He carried a torch, so clearly visible in the darkness that surrounded the rest of the Cards. He wore his red armor, a black heart slashed boldly across the chest. The gold of his crown glinted in the firelight, his eyes lit up like flames. He held the reins on the Hornhoov in one hand and his Heartsword in the other, ready to kill. He seemed to stare right at Dinah, right through her. Beside him, Cheshire sat with his dagger clutched loosely as he scanned the wood, his black, catlike eyes searching each tree, his purple cloak draped over the flank of his steed.

The Hornhoov turned her head in their direction and the king began thundering toward them. Dinah clutched the tree, pressing her face against it, fearing that her heart would actually explode.

"Stay still," ordered the voice. Dinah froze as her father's Hornhoov walked closer to them, his torch only lighting the few feet in front of him. Carefully, she raised her head and saw her father in the darkness, his face a mask of righteous fury. The king looked confused, as though he were unsure of what he was seeing. He was close enough that she could make out the sweat on his brow and smell the stink of drink clinging to his skin. She was sure he could hear her heart, which thudded with enough power to shake the tree.

Her father climbed off the Hornhoov and began making his way toward the clump of trees where Dinah was standing. Hatred flooded over her fear, and she felt an intoxicating rush of fury circle up from inside her gut. *He killed Charles*, she thought. *And I will kill him now, a shadow in the darkness. Yes, my king, come ever closer.* Moving as slowly as she could, Dinah reached for her sword, her eyes trained on his neck, the only open spot in his armor. Suddenly there was a loud crash in the woods behind her.

"There!" yelled a soldier from a distance away. "I heard something over there! I think it's her!" The king's face distorted with pleasure and he vaulted back onto the Hornhoov, turning her in the direction of the sound. Cheshire followed, giving a backward glance at the seemingly empty valley before raising his dagger menacingly and following the king. The king's Hornhoov kept trying to turn back— it could obviously smell Morte—but Dinah's father simply yanked the reins and dug his spiked heels in.

"Go, you blasted creature! Find her!" Together they galloped off into the brush, the light from his torch dimming to a dull candle in the darkness.

"Go . . . ," snapped the voice, and then Dinah heard the sound of a body dropping down from the tree above.

"Who are—"

"No time!" snapped the voice, distinctly male, somehow familiar. "Yeh, go! I'll lead them south. Quickly, for they will surely come back here." He was as invisible as she was, a hulking, dark shape in the trees. Dinah flung the bag around her, climbed onto Morte's back, and strapped the sword across her shoulders. She leaned forward and pressed herself against his black coat, becoming invisible once more. Black on black, a shadow at midnight.

"Quietly now," she whispered to her giant steed. Morte seemed to understand as they headed east, his hooves gently kissing the earth. They moved far away from the roaming Cards, deeper and deeper into the night, until the sounds of her father's army were no more. They walked quietly for hours, and Dinah noted that the flat floor of the forest was now increasingly sloping upward, harder and rockier. Hornhoov and rider moved soundlessly through the trees until Dinah spotted a small rock outcropping perched upon a narrow ridge overlooking the forest. Strategically, it would be a great place to watch for the approaching Cards, and besides, the trembling in her legs reminded her that they should go no farther. Without a word, she slipped off Morte and collapsed against the rocks, exhausted from her ride and from the all-encompassing fear. Morte knelt behind the rocks next to her and fell quickly into slumber, leaving her alone with the starless night sky.

Comforted by the fact that she didn't think her father's army could sneak up on them in the dark—or find them in the dark, for that matter—Dinah let her eyelids flicker closed once, twice, and then she surrendered to her voracious exhaustion. She dreamed of a deck of cards on a glass table, being played by a black glove. The hand was detached from an arm, and tiny flecks of crimson dripped across the faces on the cards as they were revealed. Hearts. Spades. Diamonds. The king. The king. The king.

Her eyes opened again in the early dawn and she woke drenched in a feverish sweat, unsure of what had awakened her so suddenly. Then she heard the click of a boot in front of her and felt a cold steel blade pressed firmly against her neck. Trembling, she raised her eyes, her black braid brushing the tip of her sword. A Spade stood before her, his massive frame blocking the sun.

"Morning, Princess."